Debi Evans

THE SECRET SOCIETY
OF
DRAGON PROTECTORS

'A Shadow in Time'

For Sophie

Debi Evans

Published by Debi Evans & John MacPherson

Cover design / illustration and chapter illustrations by John MacPherson

Published by Debi Evans & John MacPherson
Printed by the MPG Books Group Bodmin and King's Lynn

Copyright © Debi Evans & John MacPherson 2007
Cover design & all illustrations Copyright © John MacPherson 2007

ISBN 978-0-9554661-2-0

Contents

For Rose, who cast her own very special shadow in time.

Chapter 1

'Weaker Prey'

Angus knew exactly where he wanted to be and fought for height, furiously beating his great wings and straining their bat-like membranes almost to breaking point. The cloud base loomed ahead of his virtually vertical climb and soon he felt the refreshing dampness of the clouds encircling his scaly body. Droplets of chilled water began to run along his skin as he cut through the white layers like an arrow piercing an apple.

JN'07

1

Finally the moment Angus longed for arrived, and his dragon body leapt from the cloud like a river salmon, frozen at the apex of its jump. The cloud fell away to reveal an ethereal sea of mist before him with clear blue skies above and a brilliant sunrise bathing the whole scene in a magical light. This was the view he adored and he stayed for a moment enjoying it, flapping his wings silently in mid-air and taking in the wondrous sight before him as if time itself did not exist.

Without realising why, Angus suddenly plunged downward through the cloud and out again, spiralling toward the hills far below him. His dragon eyesight had already picked out the field he wanted and all his thoughts tuned into the flock of sheep grazing unsuspectingly on the lush grass below. As he closed in, Angus could smell their fear, as their instincts warned them that something was wrong and sent them scattering in several directions in a vain effort to evade a predator they could not yet see.

Already he had picked out a ewe that was older than the rest and had a limp causing it to run more slowly. Without malice or unkindness Angus swooped down on his prey and with one incisive and merciful bite, brought an end to the hunt, as the reproachful bleating of the other sheep rang out around the hillside.

Angus sat bolt upright in bed as the bleating in his ears turned into the blaring of his bedside alarm clock. He tried to focus on the red numbers which flashed 0630 reminding him he had to get up for school. Reaching over with his right fore-claw, no, his right hand to switch it off, he smacked his lips still tasting blood in his mouth. He stretched his wings… 'His arms!' he corrected himself, and shook his head in confusion and tried to rub the sleep from his eyes. It was a dream he'd had before but this time it was different, somehow more real. Angus was positive he had been there and that he had really done all those things he dreamt of, but sure enough here he was, sitting up in his own bed. He swung his feet onto the floor and fell over as he tried to fly to the bathroom.

'Perhaps walking is the best way', he thought, as he picked himself up from the carpet.

Inside the bathroom Angus brushed his teeth for the second time and inspected his fangs again. He was convinced that he had some wool stuck between his teeth somewhere but could not dislodge it. Nor had he managed to completely get rid of the metallic taste of blood despite swilling copious amounts of peppermint mouthwash. It was the ecological Kleanware brand his parents sold which Angus thought did not taste very nice. He peered hard into the mirror and screwing up his eyes

3

in concentration, he said to his reflection,

"You are Angus Munro... you are not a dragon... you are Angus Munro... you are not a dragon!"

He squeezed his eyes tightly shut and then opened them again. He was Angus Munro all right but he still felt a little bit dragon-like. Still confused he squinted at himself in the mirror, smacked his lips and decided to brush his teeth one last time.

Angus made his way clumsily downstairs to breakfast, his limbs still confused as to their capabilities. He proceeded to eat a very ordinary and reassuringly human bowl of cereal, despite not feeling very hungry. The headache he'd had since waking up finally started to clear and his mum was already fussing over his lunchbox while his dad had a load of Kleanware orders spread out on the kitchen table.

"You look tired dear... didn't you sleep well?" asked his Mum over her shoulder.

"Mmmm... Yeah, just some weird dreams" he replied swallowing a mouthful of cereal too quickly and hoping she would not ask him to elaborate.

His parents did not really approve of his love of dragons. They knew nothing of his secret life in The Secret Society of Dragon Protectors or that his best friend was a dragon and Angus suspected that they would freak out if they ever found out.

4

Fortunately they were far too busy building their business that was Kleanware the ecological empire of the Home Counties.

"Your lunch is here… don't forget it and make sure you have your P.E. kit this time. I don't want you getting detention again!" said his Mum breaking into his thoughts.

"Okay Mum" he replied mechanically.

"Right… I'm off to the office to update the accounts" she announced as she kissed Angus on the head and his dad on the cheek.

"I'll be there in a second" mumbled his Dad through some toast and with out looking up from the orders he was checking. The office Angus' Mum referred to was in actual fact the adjoining garage, which would never see a car in it while they lived in that house. It was so full of boxes of Kleanware products he thought they were sometimes supplying the whole of Britain and not just the few villages and towns within their county. He got up and grabbed his lunch to shove into his backpack.

"Bye Dad!" He called into the kitchen and received the normal grunt that passed for a conversation with his Dad. He banged the front door shut and set off for school.

During the familiar walk to Kynton, Angus let his mind wander. It had been a few weeks since the Trial of The Cor

Stan and he ran his mind over the adventures he and Pyrra had been through. A lot had happened in the last year and he was immensely proud to be part of the SSDP and most importantly to him, being Pyrra's protector. They had experienced many things together and during the Trials had managed to forge a mental link. They could not read each others thoughts however it was possible to sense what the other was feeling. In one trial in Krubera back in July, Pyrra had been blindfolded and the only way to navigate through the cavern was for her to somehow use his eyes and feelings, trusting each other enough to steer through a labyrinth of pillars, deep in the underground cave system that was Krubera.

This last thought brought back the dream from last night in all its colourful clarity. 'Was I really hunting last night?' he thought. He could not recall seeing Pyrra in the dream. Now that he considered it for a moment, he had been experiencing strange dreams since before the Trials, starting with the dream he shared with the dragons. He was the only one spoken to by name, which was strange as he had never met Barfoot, the previous Ward. From the discussions they had, Angus remembered that Pyrra did her hunting mostly at night or early morning, but he had never been with her on any of those bloody, but very necessary, forays for live meat. Angus had not

6

actually witnessed her going in for the kill but guessed it would look similar to what had happened in his dream. He had not told anyone about sharing the dreams with the dragons or about the message from Barfoot. Angus resolved to tell Pyrra about it the next time they met after all she was his best friend. He was hoping for a visit up to Calmor to see Rathlin and Miss Puttick, now Mr and Mrs Tek as he had not visited the island since the Trials. Angus was keen to see whether the former librarian, now mistress of Calmor, ever did manage to sort out the Tower Room files, most of which had been accumulated by the former head of the SSDP, Finian Tek. New dragons were being awakened all the time, from the Great Hibernation which had kept them safely concealed for centuries. They were being carefully monitored by the revived Secret Society of Dragon Protectors. Finian's brother, Rathlin Tek was now the head, running things from Calmor Castle on a remote island in the Irish Sea, which had recently become a dragon sanctuary once more.

Angus kicked a stone along the path absently counting the hits. 'Ten kicks without it going in the road and I'll do okay in my maths test today' but his heart sank when he saw Daniel Blake and his cronies perched on the fence, just out of view of the school gate. Daniel Blake ruled the playground at Kynton

Comprehensive. Angus hoped that the bigger boys would not see him or that they would at least leave him alone. He wished he could become invisible and slip by unobserved as it was not in Angus' nature to look for confrontation and his Mum had always told him to walk away from trouble. He did not like bullies and although braver than he realised, he kept his head down, gaining on the gate with every silent step. However, luck was not on his side and Blakey, as he preferred to be known, jumped down and blocked his path. Angus stepped to the side but the others surrounded him, jostling, jeering and trying to trip him up.

"Well then what's your hurry… stay and have a chat with us!" Blakey sneered.

"No thanks Daniel I don't want to be late" replied Angus curtly.

"Now you know I don't like anyone calling me that" growled Blakey angrily, "I think I might have to teach you some respect Dragon Boy"

The bully grabbed Angus' bag containing his precious dragon sketches as the others sniggered their encouragement. They held Angus as the larger boy pulled his shirt along with the strap of the bag giving the young protector an excellent close up of the boy's face and his acne covered skin.

"Gerroff me!" roared Angus in reply, but it was not much use against four assailants.

Blakey started emptying paper and books all over the path, encouraged by the circling vultures. That was when Angus shouted out in a hopeless attempt to stave off the senseless attack. He knew from previous experience that this was futile but this time something weird happened. The most extraordinary sound came from his mouth.

"RRRRAAAAAAAGGHHHH" cried Angus.

That was what he said but although the noise came from his mouth it originated much deeper than that. It was unrecognisable as being made by a human voice and was more like a primeval roar, if such a thing could be possible.

The bullies stopped in their tracks, completely thrown off their stride by the fearsome sound. Even Angus was stunned at what he had just done, but wherever it had come from the shock of the roar had given Angus an advantage. He quickly gathered his wits together as the other boys looked confused and snatched his bag back. Blakey, however, was not the smartest of lads and still had hold of Angus by the collar of his shirt. The bully gave a sharp tug to pull his victim off balance and seeing his prey trying to get away, aimed his fist at Angus' face. Gathering powers he did not know he had, Angus ducked

9

with surprising ease under the oncoming knuckles. In fact the bully's arm seemed to be moving in slow motion. Blakey, wrong footed, stumbled on the pavement and spun around, landing on his bum.

Blakey's accomplices could barely suppress their laughter at their foolish looking leader. Not surprisingly the bully had let go of Angus. In a last futile gesture as he picked himself up from the ground, Blakey kicked the drawings over the path and stormed off scowling in the opposite direction of school. His cohorts followed on meekly behind, having heard the unnatural sound from Angus and witnessed him make their leader look so foolish; they had suddenly lost their bravado.

Angus stooped to pick up his drawings. They were a bit scuffed, but no real harm done. He smoothed them against his shirt. His throat hurt from the strain of that roar but he grinned at the thought that he had got the better of Blakey and his mates. How, he was not sure, but this was turning out to be a strange day and he'd had his fair share of those recently. Just then, the bell sounded and Angus, only slightly ruffled from the encounter, entered school with a huge grin on his face. Blakey and company were marked absent in the register on that first September Friday back in school. No doubt they would be somewhere they should not be, causing trouble; but, unlike the sheep in his dream, Angus was not the weaker prey.

Chapter 2

'Dark Intruders'

Just as Angus was getting into bed on Friday night, an almost imperceptible dark speck appeared on the moonlit, but still foreboding, skies above Georgia.

Very slowly, the dot became more and more detailed as it neared the mountains. The first noticeable thing was the wings that shone in the moonlight as they beat rhythmically but silently, propelling the beast towards its destination. No details could be seen as the night sky seemed to absorb most of the light, allowing the darkened shape to land unseen on the harsh mountainside. Clouds spun overhead as the freezing winds drove them out towards the vast body of water that was the Black Sea.

Like a living shadow, the shape shifted one way then the other as it checked to make sure it had indeed arrived unobserved as intended. Moving swiftly, with stealth and grace unusual in something of that size, the shadow moved towards a more sheltered spot to maintain its concealment. Only when the dark mass had almost completely vanished did a smaller figure appear sitting upright on the beast's back for the first time. The person carefully dismounted, avoiding the moonlit areas of the clearing and made their way almost imperceptibly towards a clump of bushes a short distance away. Once inside, the intruder placed an odd looking pair of goggles over their eyes before replacing the hood over their head. No features could be seen as a type of face mask covered the mouth and nose. Without the aid of any visible light, the darkly clad figure walked quite confidently into the cavern.

Finian Tek, the twin brother of Rathlin Tek, who lived secretly amongst the dragons, made his way athletically up the mountainside. The robes he had chosen to wear during his many years living at Krubera, billowed around him as the wind whipped at the heavy material. He was humming to himself happily despite the inclement weather conditions and was elated at how strong and healthy he felt. He pushed onwards as he thought of his formerly estranged brother, who had come back to him, having taken over the role as head of the SSDP. He had never been more proud of his younger sibling and they now kept in touch regularly having been brought together by an outstandingly brave young man. In fact Angus Munro never ceased to amaze the former head of the SSDP and he was aware of great things ahead for Angus. The lad had an insatiable appetite for adventuring and it seemed he could not be diverted once a notion took him. Finian paused and looked up at the familiar peaks before him. He adjusted the rucksack

of supplies he had procured from the nearest town and made ready to complete the short distance to the cave entrance. Just as he took his first step he froze as a slight movement caught his eye. The shadows on

the outer edge furthest from his position hid something…
something lurking in the darkness. As he watched, the shadow
seemed to slowly move, and half a dragon head materialised.
Reflected moonlight lit the teeth and exhalations of breath,
giving an eerie and menacing glow to the form before it
stealthily drifted back into non-existence.

Below the surface, the cloaked figure entered the dragon
caves through the shimmering wall that hid the vast network of
tunnels the dragons had named the Birthing Caves. A black
gloved hand removed the goggles which had a military look to
them, revealing cold dark eyes shaded still further by the black
hood of the cloak. Frozen like a statue, the person seemed to
be listening for any sign of life and after a few moments silence
they began to slowly, and extremely quietly, move down the
tunnel towards the source of the glowing blue light now
permeating every inch of wall that was visible. Keeping to the
walls, the silent intruder passed the mirror lake without as much
as a glance at the beautiful scene which usually overawed any
visitor. Indeed it was clear that this was no guest, because any
proper caller would have announced their presence to the
occupants by now.

Only The Watcher observed the antics of the uninvited
guest as he spied on the dragon that waited impatiently

outside. The reason Finian knew this, was the evidence of seeing the nose appear in the moonlight from time to time as the dragon glanced around and shifted uneasily in the darkness.

Godroi stopped for a second and turned his head towards the entrance of the mirror cave as he left the Cor Stan. It had seemed to him that someone was there, but he could not see anything and assumed it was just his tiredness. He did not like it when Finian left the caves, as man and dragon had become very close since Godroi's victory at the Trials had proclaimed him as Ward and rightful successor to Ward Barfoot. After a few seconds he turned and lumbered towards the inner caves where some visiting dragons were resting. As the golden dragon disappeared from sight, the trespasser shifted from the hiding place they had ducked into. The Ward had almost discovered the intruder and it had visibly shaken the infiltrator. After waiting for some minutes, the figure stood once more and removed a black bag from the inside of the cloak they wore before completing the task and fulfilling the purpose of the visit.

Finian had been waiting for about fifteen minutes and was about to confront the dragon lurking in the shadows when his attention was drawn back to the entrance of the caves. He decided to stay hidden and he watched as a black clad human ran towards the waiting dragon. Once the figure reached the shadowy hiding place, the human jumped on the restless back of the dragon with ease, balanced a bag in front of the pommel on the dragon saddle and secured it in place. Dragon and accomplice took to the skies unaware that they had been detected. The keen pair of eyes that watched their departure could not identify the intruders, as the cloud cover had blanketed their escape in darkness.

The Watcher stood up and observed their escape until even his sharp eyes could no longer make them out. It started to drizzle as a precursor to yet another downpour and Finian, gathering his bundles, turned to report what he had witnessed to Ward Godroi.

Chapter 3

'Truths Uncovered'

On Saturday morning after a good, and dragon-free, night's sleep, Angus slipped out of the house and cycled to Piggleston to meet up with his dragon friend. She loved her chosen place of Hibernation, a children's ride outside Mrs James' sweetshop. Pyrra enjoyed hearing the squeals of delight as they rode on her back. She was very pleased to see Angus that morning especially when she heard the rustle of the paper bag. He fed her with her favourite cough candy unobserved by anyone in the high street.

"Hi Pyrra!" he called, but not too loudly, just in case the last retreating customer overheard him talking to a mechanical ride!

"Mmmm… Hello Angus" was the slightly muffled reply as she swallowed the sweet he had placed in her mouth.
He had often wondered how she managed to eat it since she was morphed into the ride but that discussion could wait for another time.

"No thanks" she said as he offered her a replacement for the sweet she had just devoured. "I just ate two nights ago so I'm feeling pretty full."

"Really?" he replied with interest, "were you out hunting?"

"Well if you could call it that!" she replied sadly. "It is hardly what I would call a hunt, chasing after half lame farm animals!" she finished despondently.

"Was it an old ewe you caught… with a limp?" added Angus so quietly he could barely be heard and he squirmed as he knew exactly what that entailed.

No sound came from the head of the dragon ride for a few seconds and Angus was beginning to think that she had not heard him. Just as he was about to say it again she answered.

"That was an interesting statement my friend and I can see you have something to tell me" she replied, "perhaps we should discuss this further at the trees" she concluded.

Wordlessly Angus nodded, and placing the sweets into his pocket he strode off in the direction of the small clump of trees further down the road. They had met there many times and it allowed them to talk quietly. Pyrra could not be seen but someone might still overhear them talking.

As he walked he tried to focus on what to tell her. Obviously she had to know about the dream but he was not sure about the incident with Blakey. After some inner dialogue he decided not to tell her about his newly discovered powers or the incident with the bullies. Knowing Pyrra she would want to fly round to the school and scorch them!

That thought was actually quite tempting, but Angus was content in the knowledge that he'd handled the situation well enough by himself. He also was not sure how to broach the discussion just yet and felt that the dream would cause enough of a stir. He thought he'd been with her at first, riding on her back, but now he was not so sure. He had been the dragon, felt the emotions and experienced the flight with limbs, wings, claws and teeth! Somehow he had connected with Pyrra and that connection between both of them had steadily increased since the Trials. The culmination of this was that he had somehow managed to lock into her mind in his sleep. Angus remembered he had not looked down on her streamlined flying body. He had felt the great wings as they flapped, soared and dipped. Worse still, he had actually been hunting, or at least felt as though he had. He knew that they were becoming close but this was ridiculous. He held up a hand in front of his face and turned it over slowly examining it curiously.

'This is stupid' he thought to himself. 'What am I expecting to find… claws'?

Before he realised it he was at the trees and Pyrra stood before him morphed back to her normal full size. Visible only to him, her protector, she patiently waited for him to start the conversation knowing that he would only tell her when he was

ready. Angus took a deep breath,

"Okay, on Thursday night I had a weird dream… it's a little hard to explain" he stammered.

Pyrra just stood patiently knowing that he needed no encouragement and would continue when he was ready.

"I dreamt I was flying through the air like a dragon!" he blurted out.

"What's so strange about that?" asked Pyrra quizzically.

"I was… well… flying through the clouds and then I dove on some sheep" now he had her attention, "then I caught one of the sheep and ate it!"

Pyrra stood thoughtful for a second or two before replying.

"So you think your dream is connected with my hunting trip?"

"Yes… well I think so… somehow, maybe" he replied.

"I'm sure it was just a coincidence Angus" she assured.

"No it's not. You need to understand, I know it wasn't a dream!" he pleaded. "I flew up through the clouds then after watching the sunrise I attacked the sheep and ate the one that had the limp! Only it wasn't me, it was you and I wasn't riding on your back." He paused as if considering his words, as if not sure of what he wanted to say. "I was you, in your mind and I could feel everything you felt, see everything you saw and taste everything you tasted!" he finished with a disgusted look on his face.

Pyrra looked dumbfounded.

"But you could not have been in my head, I would have felt it!" she speculated. "Although you describe all I did in such perfect detail so I don't doubt that you somehow know what I did" she surmised.

"I was there with you Pyrra I know it... I could taste the blood, which wasn't so nice, but the flight and the hunt... Wow that was a rush!" added Angus enthusiastically.

"My word!" she exclaimed, "I can see why you were so upset by it... We really did connect well at the Trials, didn't we?"

Angus nodded and smiled at Pyrra finally relieved to have told someone about the dream. The dragon chuckled,

"So I had a hitchhiker whilst hunting and I had no idea."

"What now?" Angus asked.

"I do not know Angus, perhaps we should speak to the Ward" she replied.

The friends agreed to go and visit Ward Godroi, the recently appointed Guardian of the Cor Stan and the wisest dragon they knew. Prior to becoming Ward, Godroi had been a close friend of Pyrra's and for centuries had hibernated in a stained glass window. He shared the church at Marnham with his old rival Argent, who hid in a gargoyle on the church roof so he could hear his beloved organ music. Argent missed his old adversary and Pyrra thought it would be a good idea to invite him on this trip. It had only been about six weeks since they saw Godroi but a reunion of the three dragons was a pleasing thought. Angus was all for this, as it would give him a chance to see his friend Georgina. She had become Argent's stand-in protector when her father the Vicar of St Georges church was busy.

Pleased to be in each others company, the four took to the skies above Marnham, bound for Eastern Europe. After a long but uneventful journey using dragon time to speed up their actual flying time, they were relieved to land in the barren landscape which surrounded Krubera. Once inside the cave system they were warmly greeted by The Watcher. Finian Tek was the man who wrote Dragonalia, the book Angus had found in the library which led him to discovering The Secret Society of Dragon Protectors. After a cave-in everyone, including his brother, assumed Finian had perished. He almost did, but was aided by Barfoot, the Ward at that time. In this way Finian

23

discovered the Cor Stan by chance, and it was the close proximity to the rock which gave the dragons their special powers. It also gave Finian the strength to survive the accident. He decided to continue to live secretly amongst the dragons and became the Ward's assistant and protector. This arrangement proved a huge asset to the Society, who monitored all hibernating dragons. They had entered into this state to protect themselves from mankind. Using special powers, dragons hid themselves in everyday dragon shaped objects until the world was once again a safe place to inhabit freely. That time was approaching, but the dragons knew they faced extinction unless they acted to avoid such fate.

Meeting Godroi once more, Angus observed how Pyrra's behaviour with the dragon had changed from visits prior to him becoming Ward. She seemed more formal with him and was certainly not the flirty dragon he had seen before. Godroi, for his own part, had taken on the mantle of 'Ward' with true solemnity and had totally cast off his formerly frivolous ways. In fact it was Pyrra who persuaded him that he was capable of taking on the mantle of the most powerful and respected dragon in the hierarchy. Argent, his former companion, was just as boyish as ever and he seemed oblivious to the changed attitudes of his friends. Angus observed all this with great interest and was becoming quite an expert on dragon behaviour. Anyone who was watching this scene would be amused by Angus, who had his own teenage behavioural symptoms, as his composure was always challenged by the proximity of Georgina. Without the girl even being aware of the effect she had on him, Angus felt himself colour whenever she spoke to him.

Pyrra broke into his thoughts as he heard her mention to Godroi about his dreams. The Ward along with the others then patiently listened as Angus explained about the strange dreams. When he had finished Godroi looked thoughtful.

"Tell me Angus, is this the first dream you have had like this?" asked the golden dragon in great seriousness.
Angus looked at Pyrra and wished he had told her the whole story before now, as he did not want her to think that he was in the habit of keeping secrets from her.

"No, I was having dreams before the Trials" he confessed.

"Dreams or visions?" queried Godroi further.
If Pyrra was annoyed, she did not show it and for that Angus was relieved as it made the confession easier.

"Both" he answered as Finian and Georgina exchanged a 'well this is interesting' look.
The Ward urged him to continue.

"It started when you all had the dream about Barfoot… I got it as well but at first I couldn't make it out either" he explained, "but then Barfoot spoke to me and asked me to find him"

"Barfoot spoke to you directly?" asked Pyrra.

"Yes"

"I have Barfoot's knowledge passed to me Pyrra and with that some of his memories. He *did* contact Angus" confirmed Godroi.

"Why didn't you say anything before?" she asked.

"It only came to me when Angus talked about the dream" he answered before turning back to Angus. "It seems you are particularly sensitive to the Dragonore and the same influences as we dragons, Angus. Indeed, the ease of which you have tuned to Pyrra bears witness to it and I would not be surprised if you experience other unusual things happening" said Godroi knowingly.

Angus found himself unable to look into the golden dragon's eyes. They penetrated his own with such conviction he felt sure the Ward knew there was more.

"Ah I see you are holding out on us young man, please continue" encouraged Godroi.

Reluctantly Angus found himself telling them all about the encounter with the bullies and hoped he had not lost face in front of Georgina. He smiled to himself as he saw Pyrra bristle with indignation that someone might wish to harm him. Angus explained all about the roar that terrified his attackers and the ease with which he dodged the fist. At the end of his confession Ward Godroi and Finian exchanged knowing glances.

"I am sure all is fine but what you said to those boys, although remarkable, was not very nice. Where on Earth did you learn such a word?" asked Godroi.

With a hint of his old self showing, he gave Pyrra a wry look and it was obvious who he thought was to blame. Angus did not want to say and was trying to think up a suitable answer.

"That would have been me" answered Pyrra quietly and looking thoroughly ashamed. "But I did not expect a human to be able to remember it, let alone say it!" she said, smiling at Angus. "How could you recall that, of all things?"

"Yeah Angus you're full of surprises today!" laughed Argent.

"Eh… it just came out! I didn't mean to say it and I still don't know what it means!" he replied sheepishly, trying to avoid Georgina's smirking face.

"And you won't be told the meaning by me either, I am so embarrassed that you heard me call Fergus that!" added a mortified Pyrra.

"Don't worry Angus, I will tell you later!" teased Argent. Everyone laughed at Pyrra's discomfort and Georgina seemed impressed with the way Angus had dealt with the bullies, which made him feel a whole lot better about the incident.

As they discussed the things that had happened to Angus, Finian called out for everyone's attention.

"We also have some important news for you all… we need your help with a little problem we have encountered recently" added Finian mysteriously.

With a nod of approval from Godroi, Finian continued.

"We have been subjected to some unsolicited visits" he said as the visitors looked on seriously, "someone has been helping themselves to the Dragonore!"

"What do you mean by someone, a dragon?" asked Argent.

"Not exactly… A human was responsible for the actual theft but it was a dragon that brought them here and helped them get away" he answered.

"Do you know who the person was?" asked Georgina.

"Unfortunately no, and I cannot even say if they were male or female" replied The Watcher sadly.

"What about the dragon, did you see it?" quizzed Angus who Pyrra could see was particularly enthusiastic about this new revelation. 'He see's another adventure coming on!' she mused to herself.

"I tried, but I couldn't see them properly, we guess it was Dragonore they were after and it does look as if some patches of the cave floor in the Cor Stan's chamber are barer than before" he answered pointing towards the nearby cave.

"So, do you suspect Fergus?" asked Pyrra reading Angus' mind and guessing what was on Godroi and Finian's.

"Yes we do, but who his accomplice is we do not know. Which brings us to something we need your help with" he said to Pyrra and Angus. "We need you to track down Fergus and question him. Find out if he is still involved with Felspar."

"No problem we can do that" replied Angus, "but what do we do if we find Felspar?"

"You must come for help and we will plan our next move after that. First we need to find out if it is him and what he is up to" replied Godroi, then addressing them all. "We need everyone to look, so you must inform Rathlin and the rest of the SSDP!"

As they made their way to the surface they discussed the mysterious disappearance of the mineral. Could it be something to do with the malicious dragon Felspar who had vowed revenge on everyone? He had been caught cheating during the Trials and was subsequently beaten by Godroi. The golden dragon's first act as Ward was to forever banish Felspar from the powers of the Cor Stan because of his spiteful acts. Felspar seemed bent on revenge at their last meeting and Angus remembered the dragon's humiliating banishment. He felt sure, at the time of his disappearance, that they had not seen the last of him. Finian warned them to take great care of themselves and also to pass on his brotherly greetings to Rathlin at Calmor. Now Angus had the excuse he needed to suggest a trip to the dragon sanctuary the following day. Argent and Georgina declined the invitation to join them as Georgina had a tennis match and Argent wanted to listen in on a favourite organ recital.

Back at the Cor Stan, the Ward paused for a moment gathering his thoughts until Finian broke into them.

"So what do you really think about this theft?" he probed, believing the Ward knew more than he was willing to say in public.

"My friend, we have both witnessed the unauthorised removal of vast quantities of Dragonore but we do not know who is stealing it or for what purpose. We must wait to see what happens next" was the diplomatic reply.

Finian felt frustrated and angry in the face of this wisdom but had been amongst dragons long enough to know that the Ward's decree was final. He would just need to be patient however they also had another issue that now needed to be discussed.

"What about Angus?"

"Yes I was just thinking about that... very interesting indeed... It would seem his reaction is taking place quicker than we thought... perhaps he is after all" was the strange reply.

"Who is this 'We' and 'What is he' exactly?" Finian replied looking confused. "What are you not telling me Godroi?"

Chapter 4

'Fergus'

Argent and Pyrra flew back home steadily and quietly westward away from Krubera. Angus watched the grey water below; not really taking notice of the boats that went about their daily business, totally unaware of the two large dragons flying above them. He was deep in thought, trying to understand the events that had been happening since his vision. He had ruled it out as a dream as soon as Pyrra confirmed what he already knew. He had connected with her mind without her knowing it, and as disturbing as that was, the thought was also very exciting. The experience had been thrilling to say the least, but to think it was real, and that he could possibly do it again was still more fantastic.

"Penny for your thoughts?" enquired Pyrra quietly.

"Oh… sorry was I that obvious?" replied Angus.

"You forget… I can also sense your feelings. Are you okay?" she replied.

Angus looked over at Georgina who seemed to be deep in thought with Argent. When she saw him she waved to him with a warm smile. Angus returned the gesture.

"Yes… I was just thinking about the vision I had… I wish I

knew how I did it" he replied.

"So do I… Especially since you found a way into my mind without my sensing it" she turned and smiled at him, "I must be getting old!"

"No way, you're just a young thing Pyrra!" laughed Angus at the 2000 year old dragon.

They flew on for sometime, enjoying the warmth of companionship they felt for each other. Angus believed nothing could break the bond they had, but then he thought of Felspar and his mood darkened slightly.

"Pyrra, do you think Felspar is involved in the thefts?" he asked.

The green dragon remained silent for a moment, the only sound coming from her wings as they beat rhythmically on the air currents.

"Unfortunately I do, but I hope I am wrong" she said. Angus thought the same and when it was apparent neither wanted to discuss any more, he lay his head on her back and closed his eyes.

Some hours later they dropped gently onto the lawns outside St George's church in Marnham. Pyrra spoke with Argent and Angus went to say goodbye to Georgina.

"Be careful Angus" she said as she jumped up and pecked

his cheek, instantly causing him to blush. "Don't take any chances just in case it is Felspar. You know he's dangerous!"

"I won't, and anyway I have Pyrra" he replied cheerfully and trying to sound brave.

Their goodbyes over, the two intrepid friends were soon heading home.

The next day, Angus watched as they passed over the mountains of Wales, flying towards the coast. The islands, which made up the Maidens, soon came into view and Pyrra began her now familiar approach to the castle.

They could see Cyru sunning himself in a patch of Blue Dragon Fire and he looked up just as Pyrra dove towards the ground in what looked like a certain crash landing. However she flicked out her wings and halted almost perfectly in mid-air, just a foot or two above the grass. Angus had been ready for it as it was now her trademark landing, otherwise he would have been unceremoniously thrown from her back.

Rathlin and Aurora appeared from the side of the castle as they had seen their arrival from the window upstairs. Angus could see that Mrs T still wore her tweed outfits with sensible shoes, but tended to leave her hair down more often. This was Rathlin's preference since their wedding day last April. She had been the librarian at Angus' local library and had been roped into one of his adventures. In fact he had been the one responsible for bringing them together and it was hard for him not to think of her as Miss Puttick.

"Angus my boy, how are you?" asked Rathlin as he shook hands heartily.

"Fine!" was all he could think to say.

"Angus dear what a lovely surprise!" cried Aurora as she hugged him.

"So Pyrra what brings you to Calmor on this sunny day? It must be a few weeks since we last saw you both. What news do you have?" he enquired enthusiastically.

"Hello Rathlin… I will let Angus tell you that, as I am going to have a lie down… it's been a long flight" she replied before giving a nod to the Teks and sauntering off.
She quickly made herself at home amongst the Blue Dragon Fire plant growing freely and uniquely on the rocky landscape of Calmor. She lay down next to Cyru and chatted quite happily to the islands resident blue dragon.

"Long flight… Seems to me you have a story to tell us Angus, better come inside for some tea and biscuits eh?" added Rathlin as he gestured towards the sunshine bathed walls of the old castle.

Angus sat comfortably on one of the large soft sofas that

now surrounded the fireplace. This was yet another sign of a woman's touch being present within the stone walls of the ancient Tek residence. In between mouthfuls of homemade flapjacks Angus explained about the thefts from Krubera and the request from Godroi and Finian. He did not forget to pass on Finian's regards for his brother as he helped himself to another biscuit.

"So they think its Felspar do they?" asked Rathlin immediately suspicious.

"They're not sure but we have to rule it out by first visiting Fergus and then trying to track Felspar down" replied Angus, through yet another mouthful of flapjack.

"But surely he can't do anything to Godroi now, can he?" chipped in Aurora.

"We don't know that dear… he still could be dangerous and Finian is right to start searching for him… I will spread the word to all the dragons and see if anyone has seen him" he said,

"It was just as well you went to Krubera on a social visit or we would not have known this so quickly" added Mrs T.

"Well it wasn't exactly social" replied Angus reluctantly. Soon he was coaxed into telling them all about the vision he had and the side effects afterwards.

"Well I never!" was all Rathlin could muster in reply.

"But this is terrible Rathlin, Angus may be sick we have to get him examined!" she cried.

"We can't do that dear, and he does seem fine... don't you lad?" he asked.

"I'm fine..." he confirmed, then seeing the concern on Mrs T's face, "Honest I am... It was kind of cool really, apart from the taste of blood!" he added honestly.

"Well my boy you certainly never cease to surprise... what's next, horns and wings?" joked Rathlin.

"Rathlin no, you can't say that. You will scare the living daylights out of him!" exclaimed Aurora.

Angus just laughed as he thought that would be very cool but Rathlin's reaction was funnier as he tried to make amends and stay in his wife's good books. It was not that long ago that the pair had been enemies due to Rathlin's attempt to pervert the SSDP for his own devious use in the absence of his brother Finian. Only Angus had managed to avert a disaster for the hibernating dragons by intervening. Rathlin returned to the true historical values of his family and revived The Secret Society of Dragon Protectors and made Angus the first new protector for many years.

After finally making up with Mrs T again Rathlin returned to the business at hand.

"It's getting late now, so I think we will pay a visit to Fergus next week. I will call you if any of the dragons report anything back and to arrange where we will meet."

Pyrra, despite having flown a fair distance that weekend, was now at the peak of her strength. Since her Awakening she had been fortified not only by spending time amongst the Blue Dragon Fire at Calmor, which boosts all dragons' sense of well being, but she had also benefited from her trips to Krubera. Being close to the source of all dragons' power gave them more energy. The Cor Stan literally recharged her batteries and she did not balk at the suggestion of yet another long flight in such a short time.

Angus was actually enjoying a trouble free time at school and his teachers noticed a positive enthusiasm about the boy's study, especially in his Art classes where he still included a dragon in every picture. Daniel Blakey and his gang had not bothered him lately. When they actually deigned to turn up at school they took the trouble to stay out of his way. He noticed one day at home time that they were hanging around near the school gate and when one of them saw him, they nudged Blakey. Angus braced himself for the inevitable, but was surprised when Blakey got up and walked off in another direction, shouting at some other boy he intended to pick on.

Later, when he thought about it, Angus recognised the look of fear on Blakey's face just before the bully had selected another victim and went after a boy from 8D.

The week past by quickly as Angus and Pyrra made several visits to the dragons they knew. They visited Argent three times, which Angus was always keen to do, and more pleasing, Georgina seemed happy to see him also. He had told her about the impending visit to Fergus and she expressed her eagerness to go. Angus agreed to call her and let her know, once Rathlin had divulged the plans. Between the visits, his homework and his parents' Kleanware deliveries he was kept extremely busy and soon the weekend loomed again.

Placing his bike against the wall of the house, Angus entered the house through the back door and walked into the kitchen. He had just been to the library for a book and still found it strange not to find Miss Puttick, now Mrs Tek, behind the desk. His Mum was busy preparing dinner with the radio on and had not heard him come in.

"Hi Mum!" he called to her as he walked past. "What's for tea?" he asked hoping it was not pasta again.

"Angus! Don't sneak up on me like that!" she exclaimed.

"But I didn't!" he pleaded innocently.

"Well you need to make more noise like a normal

teenager... I swear you seem to move around like a ghost at times!" she replied. "Now go do your homework and wash up... and yes we are having Lasagne!"

Angus sloped off upstairs with his book thinking that the dinner choice could have been worse, as at least he liked Lasagne. His Mother was not strictly correct as Angus was not thirteen yet. His birthday was still four weeks away and far from his mind at the minute. He finished his Geography homework and had no sooner finished drying his hands when the phone rang.

"I'll get it!" he shouted and ran to the table in the hallway downstairs.

"Hello Angus, it's Rathlin" replied the head of the SSDP after Angus answered. "Can you meet me tomorrow at nine a.m. at Long Reach?"

"No problem Rathlin... Can I bring Georgina?" asked Angus casually.

"Of course, that's a good idea. Her presence might make the situation less confrontational" answered Rathlin. "See you there then!" he finished.

Angus replaced the receiver and dialled Georgina to let her know the details before going into the kitchen for dinner. Now he had to make up a good excuse for his parents so as to avoid being roped into more Kleanware chores.

As arranged Pyrra with Angus, met Georgina and Argent at Marnham Church early before flying onward to Long Reach. Rathlin stood in the garden of the old house waiting with Cyru. The house looked better than before as some restoration work had been done at the insistence of Aurora. She did not intend to spend the harsh winters on the island at Calmor as the Irish Sea could be very rough at that time of year. The poplar trees still divided the grounds and Angus recalled how Pyrra had practiced her flying skills for the Trials to great effect here. Soon they were off to London and landing in the park near where Fergus lived.

As Angus jumped down from Pyrra's back Rathlin walked over to speak to him.

"I think you had better go up alone while Georgina and I wait here… His Mother may be in and it will look more natural and less alarming if it's just you" he said.

Angus nodded in agreement, although he did not know what kind of reception he would receive from the older lad. They had parted company six weeks ago after Fergus and Felspar had been caught cheating during the Trials. The unfortunate protector had been misled by the black dragon and coerced into helping Felspar cheat. On discovery, he had been banished from the SSDP for ever, but Angus still felt a little sorry for the lad and hoped that Fergus would not be bitter about the past.

The young protector knocked on the door and when the boy opened it, Angus was surprised that Fergus did not look anywhere near as tall and lanky as he remembered him, but then he had probably grown himself. The older lad had obviously filled out a bit and had stubble on his chin that Angus could not boast. He still wore the worn looking black jeans and rock band t-shirt that Angus remembered seeing him in before. Fergus looked surprised at first and looked around Angus for any companions, then realising that the younger lad was alone, he relaxed a little.

"Hi... so what brings you here then?" was the dry greeting.

"We need to talk to you Fergus... Rathlin and Georgina are over the road" replied Angus quickly, eager to have this part of his task over with, "We didn't want to scare your Mum!" he added.

Fergus seemed to consider the request before answering.

"Let me get my trainers on!" he said before closing the door and leaving Angus outside.

Fergus walked to Rathlin with Angus almost jogging to keep up, the long strides of the taller lad forcing him to do so.

Rathlin extended his hand and Fergus reluctantly shook it, avoiding eye contact with the head of the SSDP.

"Angus tells me you want to discuss something with me?" he asked guardedly.

"Yes Fergus... I'm sorry lad... it's about Felspar... we need your help" replied Rathlin hesitantly as if not sure how to approach the situation.

"*You* need *my* help?" replied Fergus in disbelief. "How can I help you, I'm no longer a protector, remember?"
Angus could hear the bitterness in the older lad's voice and he could not blame him. He only had to think of how he would feel had he been banished from seeing any dragons ever again.

"Please Fergus... It's really important" interjected Georgina. At the sight of the girl the tall lads face mellowed slightly and his demeanour changed.

"Oh... Hi Georgina. Sorry I didn't see you there" he answered softly. "How are you?"

"I'm fine" she smiled, "but if you could listen to what we have to say and help us in any way you can, we would appreciate it" she added a little more seriously.
Rathlin suppressed a smile, thinking it had been a good thing to bring Georgina after all.

"Perhaps you can explain, Georgina?" he encouraged,

keeping a straight face.

"We need to know where Felspar is… do you know?" she asked.

"I honestly don't know… or care for that matter! He caused me so much grief I don't want anything to do with his stupid plans!" he finished.

Angus realised from the reply that Felspar had been in touch. Perhaps they would be lucky and he hoped that Georgina had picked up on the fact also.

"Has he been here then?" she asked quickly.

"Yeah, he came round about three weeks ago asking me to help him… he wanted to get some Dragonore and needed me to get it for him" replied Fergus.

Rathlin and Angus stirred as it looked like they had come to the right place for the proof they needed.

"Where did he plan to get the Dragonore?" probed Georgina.

"He didn't say… just that he needed it and I could help" replied the tall lad. "I wish I knew more but that's all I can tell you."

At first Angus could not decide whether Fergus was unwilling or unable to tell them any more about his former charge but he decided the older boy was telling the truth.

"I have kept my promise to you Rathlin... I won't have any more to do with Felspar" the older boy insisted. "I didn't really take much notice of his boasting and I don't know anything more than I've told you... sorry but I just told him I wasn't interested in any journeys, wherever it was he wanted me to go."

Angus and the others took their leave of the sorry looking lad not wanting to bother him any longer than was necessary.

"If he comes back lad, make sure you call me... here's my number just in case" said Rathlin giving Fergus a card as they prepared to depart.

"When you find him be careful... he's as mad as ever!" warned Fergus. "He wants revenge on everyone, especially you and Pyrra" he added looking at Angus.

"Thanks, we will" replied Angus shaking the tall lad's hand. They had not really learned anything new and were about to take off when Fergus suddenly called them back.

"Wait! There was something!" shouted Fergus. "He boasted about something he had found... but I didn't know what it meant."

"Try to remember! It might be important!" pushed Rathlin eagerly.

"I'm trying!" exclaimed Fergus. "It was something about a

door" he continued softly, "but that's not the right word."

"A door?" repeated Rathlin. "That could mean anything… are you sure that's right?"

"No it was another word… if only I could remember it… PORTAL!" he shouted triumphantly. "That was it… a portal of some kind!"

"Well I'm stumped by that one lad. Don't know what that crazy dragon's talking about… Anything else?" replied Rathlin, puzzled.

"He didn't tell me anything else…" replied Fergus trailing off.

"Well I thank you for your help Fergus. You may have given us something there" assured Rathlin, patting the lad's shoulder.

Fergus waved them off and they returned to Long Reach again to discuss the next move. Neither of the younger protectors knew what a portal was and Rathlin explained that it was a sort of doorway, but to what, he did not know.

"I remember some of Finian's notes mentioning a portal of some kind, but I paid it little attention" he continued, "wish I'd taken more notice now."

"Pyrra, can you remember anything about a portal?" asked Angus keen to know more.

"Alas no… I've never heard of such a thing" she replied.

"I do remember it had something to do with ancient stones and ley lines but nothing else" added Rathlin.

"What, you mean like Avebury or Stonehenge?" queried Georgina.

"Similar but not on such a grand scale as those" answered Rathlin.

"But what's that got to do with a portal?" asked Angus looking understandably confused.

"We'll have to ask Finian that one lad" he replied, "and there's no time like the present!" he added climbing back onto Cyru's back.

"But you can't go to Krubera now!" shouted Angus. "It's too late to leave today."

"Who said anything about going to Krubera?" replied Rathlin with a wink.

"But how else will you talk to him?" asked Angus confused.

"Ah wait and see lad… wait and see" he replied mysteriously.

Rathlin was anxious to speak to his brother at Krubera, and having told Angus this, the head of the SSDP now prepared to travel back to Calmor to facilitate the communication. It made no sense and Angus was dying to know how that might happen without actually going to Krubera, but Angus sensed that

Rathlin was in no mood for explanations and he and Georgina watched the man take off with Cyru. Angus sensed they were on the precipice of something great but did not know what was about to happen.

Chapter 5

'Doorways'

As Rathlin disappeared into the distance, Angus was at a bit of a loss and wondered what to do next. That was when Georgina came up with a suggestion which made him extremely happy.

"Daddy keeps this amazing ice-cream at home and I'm sure I can persuade him to part with some... would you like to come to the Rectory?" she asked shyly.

Angus had still been pondering the conundrum of how Rathlin would contact Krubera and was slightly taken aback by the invitation. However he was not so overwhelmed as to pass up the chance of spending time with someone who was becoming one of his best friends.

"Too right I would!" he replied enthusiastically. "Are you okay with that Pyrra?" he asked.

"Hope its liquorice flavour!" the dragon replied.

At that the protectors jumped up into the saddles and with a flick of their powerful wings the dragons took off in tandem, into the midday sunshine.

Meanwhile, Cyru landed at the rear of Calmor Castle at the insistence of Rathlin, who then promptly vaulted from the saddle like an over-excited teenager and strode towards the lighthouse shouting 'Thank you'. The young blue dragon thought the man had lost it again and feeling rather sleepy, decided to go to his favourite flattened spot of Blue Dragon Fire. Much to his dismay he found it occupied by Nehebkau and had to find another place which was far less comfortable.

Rathlin raced down the grassy slope at Calmor as if his trousers were on fire. He did not stop to pet his dogs that

barked excitedly and pranced about because their master was racing towards them. He knocked on the door of the small cottage that formed the base of the bright white lighthouse and burst in without waiting for an answer. The cottage contained one bedroom with a kitchen and bathroom, 'just enough for a simple man' as Dermot was fond of saying. He was the Warden at Calmor; all round general handyman and trusted by the Tek family, having been with them for some years. As far as the SSDP was concerned he was indispensable since he made sure things ran properly on the island, and tended the Blue Dragon Fire as well as keeping the human visitors fed with his famous flapjack. He sat at a small cabinet within the white washed walls of the lighthouse engrossed and confused with the contraption that lay in front of him. The room had uncomplicated furnishings that were purely functional and as Rathlin walked across the stone floor, Dermot turned to greet him.

"Ah, good afternoon to you Sir, you're a sight for sore eyes for sure" he said before pointing at the computer console on the wooden cabinet. "This thing has the beating of me!"

"I'm sorry it had to be placed here Dermot but it is the best place for a signal and with the antenna on top of the lighthouse it makes perfect sense… I'm sure you'll get the hang of it and then you can teach me how to use it!" he finished smiling.

"Chance would be a fine thing Sir" he replied sharing the joke.

"Actually, I need to use this contraption now to send an urgent message I don't suppose she has it working yet, does she?" asked Rathlin hopefully.

"Well Sir the lady would be having it working no problem but she is just making some tea, seeing as she saw your arrival... very down to earth for someone with such a privileged upbringing" was the jovial reply from Dermot.

Dermot got up and moved to one side and Rathlin seated himself at what looked like a normal laptop computer. At least on first glance it did, but once you looked closer you could see other equipment. A smaller box lay under the cabinet which was the main encryption and decoding unit. The whole thing was linked to a satellite dish that communicated with a stationary satellite orbiting high above Europe. Rathlin had been told by the benefactor donating this equipment that it was ex-military and very state of the art. He would never be able to tell the difference but he knew he would not be playing games of any kind on this piece of hardware!

The kitchen door creaked open on its hinges and Rathlin turned to see Meredith Quinton-Jones, a recent and very keen recruit, carrying in three steaming mugs of tea. It was Miss Quinton-Jones who had donated the high-tech satellite linked technology to the SSDP, to save on dragon flights and make the running of the Society from its headquarters more efficient. Rathlin rather liked the forthright young woman and admired her business acumen. She ran a small but very successful oil and gas drilling company and her injection of cash and equipment confirmed her enthusiasm and commitment to the Society. She was proving a great asset to the SSDP even though Aurora had her misgivings about the woman. Rathlin brushed these aside as petty womanly jealousies without any real foundation and had explained to his wife that she was the only woman for him.

"Thought you could do with one of these after your long flight" said Meredith as she offered Rathlin one of the mugs.

"Thanks, I didn't think anyone was around... So how is your knowledge of prehistoric sites?" he asked, accepting the mug with a smile.

"About as good as your technical skills I'm afraid..." she laughed, "Why, what have you found?"

"Oh nothing much, just something I need to report to Finian and Godroi... I think its nonsense really, but best be sure... now if I could only remember what you taught me!" he replied fiddling with various buttons on the console.

"Here let me" said Meredith reaching across him and smiling as she flicked a switch.

The screen flickered into life and after a small amount of buzzing and clicking, the whole screen lit up; prompted by the computer Rathlin typed in his password. A few moments later the face of Liam appeared on the screen. He had gone to Krubera to help set up the terminal and satellite there as he had shown a great aptitude for the technology.

"Hey Rathlin… How ya doin?" asked Liam who lived in Dublin.

"Hello Liam… well it looks like you've got things under control there… are Godroi and Finian nearby?" asked Rathlin.

"Sure they're right here… Hold on…" replied Liam before jumping out from the camera's view.

The screen seemed to move but in actual fact it was the terminal being shifted in Krubera and it made Rathlin feel a little giddy. Seconds later the unmistakable golden visage of Godroi filled the screen with Finian standing next to him.

"Well now this is a much easier way to keep in touch don't you think?" called Rathlin speaking louder than was probably necessary.

"Of course Rathers, but I hope that does not signify your

intention not to fly to Krubera to see your old brother every now and then" replied Finian warmly.

"Certainly not Fin, how could I not come and see my older sibling who is a whole three minutes older than I?" quipped Rathlin.

"Now remember Rathers, its three and a half!" replied Finian laughing.

"It is good this link appears to be working and it will be very useful indeed. We must thank Meredith" added Godroi.

"You just did" replied Meredith stepping behind Rathlin so they could see her, "and it was my pleasure" she added smiling.

"So Rathers, is this just a social visit? We gather from Liam that Angus has passed on our message" asked Finian.

"Yes he did, but we should discuss the lad later... I've got some news about Felspar!" replied Rathlin seriously.

"Okay we should discuss this in private I think!" said Finian pointedly.

"No that's fine... I understand... some things must be kept quiet until the right moment!" said Meredith in response to Rathlin's apologetic smile.

"Well now Ma'am... have you ever tried my flapjacks yet?" he heard Dermot say as the pair left the lighthouse.

Rathlin told the Ward all they had discussed with Fergus and their fear that Felspar may have found something that could harm them.

"Was the lad able to tell you what Felspar discovered?" asked Finian.

"Some sort of doorway or portal I think… Does that mean anything to you?" replied Rathlin.

"I know of the existence of a portal but neither its location nor its use comes to mind" replied Finian, sadly shaking his head. Godroi, if concerned by this news, did not display any outward sign of it. The old dragon remembered such a portal himself but could not recall much about it, other than that it was in the UK somewhere. A tardy memory is the by-product of many years spent in Great Hibernation and this curse afflicted most newly awakened dragons. "The name Stanbury springs to mind but I cannot recall why!" he added.

"I can" Finian replied.
Prior to the cave-in at Krubera where he disappeared from his earthly life, Finian had been exploring not only the source of Dragonore, but also the secrets of its magical properties.

"It's in my notes at Krubera but the document you need is probably in one of the boxes… It's very old and in poor condition but I managed to decipher some of it many years ago" he looked serious and thoughtful. "It was fantastic and I dismissed it as nonsense at the time, but now I'm not so sure."

"What did it say?" asked Rathlin eagerly.

"It spoke of time travel though portals!" replied Finian. The former head of the SSDP had learned from his intense worldwide research that it might be possible for dragons to time travel using large amounts of Dragonore, but he had not discussed this with anyone and now seemed the best time. Ward Godroi who had listened carefully spoke.

"From the inherited memories that I have had passed to me, it is possible Dragonore could actually make it possible to travel back through time. However it is usually forbidden and has rarely been used!"

"Can Felspar really know of this?" asked Rathlin.

"It would seem so and we cannot take any chances..." replied Godroi, "he must be found and stopped from doing this, if that is indeed his intention."

"It would be a good idea to find this portal for safety's sake Rathers... just as a precaution" added Finian, "Perhaps that wonderful woman you married can find it using her excellent research skills?"

"She's in Kynton at the moment checking on her cottage, but I will certainly call her and let her know" replied the head of the SSDP.

The screen flickered off as the connection was severed until the need for contact arose again. Rathlin considered that they would have to have a regular schedule of contact agreed upon but his head was full of portals and time travel. He reached behind his head, adjusted his pony tail and after finishing his tea, departed to use the phone.

Chapter 6

'Megaliths'

Back in Kynton, Aurora Tek was trying hard not to go into her former place of employment, the library. Whilst in the locality she had paid a courtesy visit to Angus' parents. In the chaotic office in their converted garage she assured them that Angus was always very well behaved on his visits to Calmor. Since she found Donald and Jeannette Munro knee deep in Kleenware orders as usual, she took her leave as quickly and as politely as possible and found herself instead drawn to the library. She had not really intended to go back to her old place of work, but was curious to peep inside and was surprised to find it open. Maybe this was an opportunity to view her successor and see just how the library was doing since her departure. Aurora stood outside the red brick building as she tried to decide if going in would be a good idea or not when Rathlin rang her mobile.

"Hello dear… How did your trip go?" she asked.

"Quite fruitful my love… In fact that is why I am calling you" he replied, "I need your help."

"Indeed…" she said, then with concern. "I hope everyone is okay!"

"Everyone is fine dear… I need you to find something out for us, can you get to the library?" he asked.

"I think I can manage to fit it in" she replied with a smile, not wishing to admit she had her nose pressed up against the window.

"Good… I need you to do some research on ancient burial sites with standing stones!"
Rathlin went on to explain all about their findings and the subsequent discussion with Godroi and Finian. She now had a reason to go inside. This was just the excuse she needed and she seized the opportunity.

Aurora felt a familiar pang of nostalgia as she pushed open the heavy glass door with it's loud 'swoosh' and breathed in the familiar air of knowledge that she so missed. As she did so, she could not help but notice that the shelves were not quite as tidy as they had been in her day. Mrs T found herself tutting at the young woman behind her desk and was it her imagination or did the girl have headphones on? The new librarian certainly seemed to be attached by the ears to a small box.

The former librarian ignored the younger woman and marched straight through to the reference section. On the local history shelf she found 'Professor Willard Saggerson's Comprehensive Guide to Prehistoric Sites in The British Isles' but was unable to find a clear desk to open the heavy book. Mrs T scooped up the discarded daily newspapers from the reading table and dramatically dumped them on the librarian's desk. The startled girl picked up the bundle of papers and stuffed them underneath. She did this while nodding her head in time to the music on her Mp3 player, managing to avoid eye contact with the crazy woman thumbing through the big dusty reference book. No one argued with Aurora Tek when she was in this sort of mood. Concentrating on the index, she fumbled in her handbag for her reading glasses, perched them on her nose and peered closely as she ran her finger down the listings. Mrs T wondered where to start. Rathlin had not given her much to go on but she seized the task, excited by the challenge.

Angus arrived home just as his Dad was about to leave to deliver some orders. He'd had a brilliant time at Georgina's house and they had talked with her Dad for ages while eating loads of a special raspberry ripple ice-cream he bought from a local shop that made their own. The vicar was actually a very funny man, although Angus suspected it was unintentional half of the time. He wondered if his parents had even noticed that he had been out all day and went into the office to let them know he was home.

Leafing through the index and enjoying the obscurity of unusual place names, Mrs T, as was her way, and to the puzzlement of everyone else, worked alphabetically backwards from Z to A. Zennor Quoit! She found the page and immediately saw a fabulous pile of stones, located in Cornwall and as she skimmed through the text, the words 'dolmen portal' leapt off the page at her. This was going to be far more fun than she had first anticipated and the thought that one of these sites could possibly transport a dragon through time was truly amazing. She began to read again with the enthusiasm of a child with a new toy.

"Mum said you'd called in… and when you weren't at home I guessed you'd be here..." panted Angus, then realising what she was doing added. "It's cool they open on a Saturday now but I don't see it lasting as no-one ever comes in… So what are you looking for, anything interesting?"

"Oooh Angus… you gave me such a fright!" she exclaimed rather too loudly, which drew a frowning look from the librarian. Aurora was affronted to be seen as a noise maker in any library but in this one, her old haunt, was just unbearable!

"Now look at that young man… you've got me in trouble!" she scolded in a loud whisper.
Angus turned and with a smile waved at the new librarian.

"Hi Mrs Fletcher… Sorry bout that… We'll keep it down!" he called across the room and causing Mrs T to roll her eyes. "Its cool Mrs T" said Angus turning to her again, "You're with me so she'll be okay" he finished grinning at her.

"I have never been so embarrassed in all my days Angus Munro!" she replied indignantly, but could not help smiling in the face of his cheek.

Aurora proudly showed Angus her discovery and he looked at the photograph.

"It kind of looks like a launch pad" he commented cocking his head to the left.

"It could also be the sort of thing they were looking for" she added and made a careful entry in her notebook.

"Don't you think the internet would probably be quicker than flicking through this big book?" he asked hopefully, but that fell on deaf ears as Mrs T liked the old fashioned method of using reference books.

"Observe and learn" she said to the frustrated lad.

Angus looked at what she was reading and picked up a word from the text and moved towards the library's free computers.

"I'll just search monoliths and see what it turns up" he said tactfully and soon he found himself on a fabulous website showing all the standing stones in the British Isles, just at the touch of a button.

"Wow here's a good one… look up Drumskinny in County Fermanagh, Ireland… that'll be under 'D'!" he added cheekily. The librarian leafed through the big book and agreed it was a fair sized stone circle.

"It's certainly worth consideration" she replied before adding it to the list. "Rathlin did mention Stanbury which I think is a town or a village but I have not come across it yet" she added.

Angus tried a word search on it but only came up with a place in West Yorkshire which gave no reference to any standing stones nearby.

"Look at this one on your computer Angus and see if you can find a picture of it… Cairnholy One in Kirkcudbrightshire, known as a Clyde Cairn… that won't be too far to check out from Calmor."

When he found it on the site it certainly looked impressive and according to the information he read it was a megalith tomb construction.

As he looked at the pictures on the screen, Aurora, with a furtive look at the librarian, read out quietly.

"The name Cairnholy may have been derived from Carn Ulaidh which means treasure cairn" she said excitedly and

Cairnholy joined the list.

"…and this one…'Devil's Den', a prehistoric barrow with standing stones" called Angus over his shoulder, not as worried about being silent in the library as Mrs T was.

They were the only two people in the building other than the librarian with the Mp3 player. She appeared to be cowering further behind her desk in an attempt to avoid any eye contact with her predecessor.

"…and Castlerigg in Northumberland… possibly one of the oldest stone circles in Europe" enthused Aurora now forgetting the no noise rule in her excitement.

"What about Avebury and Stonehenge in Wellshire?" added

Angus.

He was really getting into this, and had no idea there were so many ancient standing stones still around, until he observed all the little dots on the map in front of him.

"Rathlin thought the likely place we are looking for is smaller than those touristy sites and not so well known" cut in Mrs T, "but I'm rather fond of Wellshire and consider it to be a most magical county, right up there with Cornwall and Northumberland... let's have a look on an Ordinance Survey map and see if anything else around there looks likely" she said as she opened the map out and put her finger on Avebury and started moving it eastwards.

Her eye was drawn to a fault line of Saracen stones scattered haphazardly all the way along a valley and then she found something unusual. The valley of stones petered out and right in the middle of a field she saw the exciting word 'Megalith' written in Old English style and she knew at once that this would have to go on the list. She wondered if she might find verification in the local history books as Angus could not locate this one on his very useful website. She smiled in triumph as this proved beyond doubt, that books were more reliable at the end of the day!

Refolding the map and replacing it perfectly on the shelf,

Mrs T frowned at the librarian who was still nodding to her music and flicking through a magazine. She tried to ignore the dust as she ran her fingers along the spines of the beloved books. Eventually she found the object of her search and was pleasantly surprised to find it where it should be. Mrs T lifted down another weighty tome entitled 'Prehistoric Burial Sites and Their Importance in Ancient Britain'. Expertly flicking through the pages she soon found the Wellshire chapter, full of Stone Age, Iron Age and Bronze Age hill forts as well as barrows. There was a picture of the two lichen covered upright stones and a whole variety of ancient rocks portrayed there which she showed Angus.

"They look like ancient goalposts!" he laughed.

"I have to admit they do appear so!" she replied and made another note on her list.

They continued searching for some time, adding the most likely candidates but not finding a Stanbury.

"Here's another one, Bryn Celli Ddu on the Isle of Anglesey in Wales… A henge with a stone circle, most unusually covered by the chamber and cairn of a second monument… it resembles a small hill… what do you think?" she smiled.

They added the last few to the list and were pleased with their afternoon's work. Angus could not really see how the list could be useful in their search for the portal that Fergus spoke of.

"Finian believes it may be possible to use the portal for travelling through time!" she explained quietly.

He could not believe his ears.

"NO WAY!" he replied rather too loudly and causing the librarian to glance up. "That's awesome… is it really possible?" he whispered.

"I doubt it… it is probably just some old tale, but Rathlin and Finian do not want to take any chances" she replied.

Despite Mrs T's doubt, Angus was thrilled at the potential of this new discovery and the thought of jumping through time was a prospect he found very appealing. He had read many books and some had been about adventures involving time travel but his dreaming was interrupted by Mrs T as she plonked one of those large books in his arms to put back on the shelf and his excitement had to be contained for the moment. They left the library exactly as they found it, except possibly a bit tidier, and Angus thought he heard the librarian behind the desk expel a sign of relief as the door swished closed behind them.

Chapter 7

'Fatal Strike'

Angus and Mrs T walked towards his home talking animatedly about the various megaliths and burial chambers they had found. He pushed his bike and they reluctantly agreed that it was too late in the day to return to Calmor.

"So I will meet you in the morning then, Mrs T?" confirmed Angus.

"Yes… we can leave from my house around nine" she replied. "Now are you sure you don't want me to speak to your parents? I don't like the idea of you going off and not telling them!"

"Its okay Mrs T… they will never know and it's not like I can tell them I'm going to the Irish Sea and back in one day!" he laughed.

She knew he was right but it certainly did not sit well with her moral values. She tried to put it from her mind as just another SSDP situation she could not do anything about and at least she was keeping a watchful eye on the lad.

"I will have Tejas inform Pyrra and she can meet us at the cottage" she added, before waving goodbye.

Angus went to his back door and propped his bike against the wall before entering the house. His Dad was sleeping on the sofa with the television on and by the sounds of it his Mum was having an early evening bath upstairs. Announcing he was home to no-one in particular, he decided to read in his room for a bit before dinner.

The book he was reading was not all that interesting, but it was part of his English homework so he tried his best to stick to the task. The words started to swim around on the page and he fought a losing battle to keep his eyes open.

Pictures of the day's events filtered through his mind in a jumbled up order. He saw all manner of stones and hillsides, and then Fergus and Rathlin in conversation. More stones, Long Reach, Georgina, Pyrra and then back to the stones. From the last stones, he had a pleasant experience flying over an unfamiliar landscape. Angus focused on something below him. A linear white horse drawn on the ground, or was it a horse? It looked very much like a stick drawing of a dragon. He thought he recognised it as a place he had visited way back in primary school. It was close to an Iron Age hill fort and the name Serpent Tor spun in and out of his subconscious. His old teacher appeared and told him that the Wellshire locals believed it was the spot was where George had killed the dragon. Then he saw a dragon rolling down the sweeping grassy bank until it came to a halt at the foot of the escarpment. It was stone dead and sent up a puff of chalk as it came to a stop. A knight in armour, stood at the top with both hands raising his sword to the heavens in triumph. The light, that had not been apparent to him in the visions until it suddenly darkened, made him more alert as the images took on a much more sinister tone. A dragons head flashed in his mind for a brief moment and then the scene changed to Marnham, although some of the town was missing. His mind raced, searching for familiarity and the dragon flashed back into his head, its mouth moving but not making any sound. As abruptly as it appeared, the dark blue dragon was replaced by a battle scene, but not between humans; two dragons fought a very bloody combat. Even in his sleep, Angus recognised the dragons immediately, a golden one and a black one. The aggressor grinned manically all the while baring his ferocious teeth and definitely winning the fight. Angus was horrified to see the black dragon with the upper hand, but felt compelled to keep watching even though he was afraid of what was coming. Again the images merged and changed, as the unfamiliar dark blue dragon reappeared.

"Rescue the Ward!" was all it said and then as mysteriously as he came, was gone.

The fierce fighting resumed and Felspar had the wounded Godroi pinned against the church wall. It reminded Angus of the fight Pyrra had with Felspar and the black dragon raised his talons in the same dramatic fashion. The image of the claw swam large in his mind blocking out everything else until it vanished only to reappear covered in blood!

"NOOOOO!" shouted Angus sitting up on his bed.
Sweat poured into his eyes making them sting. He got up shakily and staggered to the downstairs bathroom feeling dizzy and disorientated. Random thoughts raced through his mind; 'Had he really just witnessed the death of Godroi? Why was he in Marnham? Who was that other dragon?' Angus turned on the tap and cupped cold water onto his face and neck trying to snap out of it.

He did not remember feeling tired and since it was only six o'clock he did not believe he had fallen asleep, yet it seemed to be a dream. 'Why do I keep having these weird dreams?' The stuff before the fight was from his memory, but the battle and the new dark blue dragon were all new. Serpent Tor was from his old primary school trip and his teacher had told him some people believed that the dragon lived beneath the hill and when it came out to fight George its fiery breath scorched away the grass leaving a pattern on the side of the hill in white chalk. Since he'd joined the Secret Society of Dragon Protectors Angus knew a very different story of George and his battle with Godroi. That brought him back to the golden dragon's struggle within the images that had darkened his mind. The dark blue dragon had spoken several times but only once did the message become clear. The voice had said 'Rescue the Ward' and Angus guessed that referred to Godroi but who that dragon was, he had no idea. At first he had thought it was Pyrra but the horns and the colour told him otherwise. The talons flashed back into his mind and he cringed at the thought of what must surely have been a fatal blow.

Angus knew he must speak to someone quickly and only stopping to shout upstairs that he was going out and to put his dinner in the oven, he sped on his bike to Mrs T's cottage. He threw his bike on the grass and rang the door bell urgently.

"Felspar killed Godroi!" he blurted out breathlessly to her as she opened the door.

"Angus!" she exclaimed, "What are you talking about?

How?" she asked, her eyes wide in shock.

"I saw Felspar kill Godroi… just ten minutes ago!" he said as she motioned him into the house.

"But I just left you thirty minutes ago and Godroi's in Krubera…"

"I know but I saw him in Marnham and Felspar was fighting with him and then the claw…" Angus tapered off.

"Calm down Angus" soothed Mrs T as she held his shoulders and sat him down on a chair. "Now tell me from the start what happened."

Angus took a deep breath and described everything in as much detail as he could remember, getting more and more agitated as he told of the fatal blow. Aurora Tek sat for a second or two looking surprised at what she had just heard. Had it been anyone else telling her she would have dismissed it by now as a simple nightmare but this was Angus and apparently his dreams or visions were not to be taken lightly.

"Let's call Rathlin right now and he can talk to Godroi to see if he is safe" she eventually said.

"But we have to go to Krubera!" replied Angus urgently.

"We have a way to make contact now which is much quicker" she replied.

"Is this why Rathlin did not go to Krubera today… What is

it?" he asked.

"Oh some satellite thingy that woman gave us!" replied Mrs T testily, "But let's call him and see if he can put your mind at rest."

Soon Rathlin was on the phone and quite taken aback by what his wife had to tell him. He immediately asked her to wait for his return call and he would speak to Godroi without delay.

Five minutes can seem a very long time when you are watching the clock tick slowly onwards with every second taking an eternity. Angus paced up and down, checking the clock time and time again, his face etched with worry. Mrs T found herself nibbling on a fingernail which was something she had not done in years and was annoyed with herself for doing so. The phone rang causing both of them to jump.

"Hi Angus… I thought you might answer" said Rathlin after Angus had grabbed the phone before Mrs T could even stand up.

"Is he okay?" asked Angus immediately.

"Ask him" was the reply, "he can hear you… I have a mobile on loudspeaker… handy thing this… might get one myself…"

"Godroi are you okay?" shouted Angus over Rathlin's babbling.

"Of course I am Angus, why would I be anything else?" was the quieter and tinny sounding reply from the Ward.

"I saw you being hurt by Felspar and I thought…" Angus' voice trailed off as he realised how foolish he must sound.

"What did you see Angus?" asked Godroi.

"Lots of stuff but I saw you fighting Felspar and he…"

"Go on" urged Godroi.

"It must have been a dream… but I saw him kill you!" replied Angus eventually.

"He cannot harm me here in Krubera Angus and I am most unlikely to leave. Tell me exactly what you remember" replied the golden dragon encouragingly.

Angus relayed the events of his dream again. He tried to remember all the details but already some of the images were lost to him. Godroi stopped him from time to time gently confirming points of the dream. The Ward was deeply touched by the boy's concern but did not want him to worry unduly.

"I gather you will be in Calmor tomorrow and we will speak to each other then" said the Ward.

That said, Angus replaced the receiver, and after informing Mrs T of what Godroi had said, he made his way home for dinner feeling a bit happier.

Angus slept quietly that night and the next morning he and

Mrs T raced back to Calmor as fast as their dragons could carry them. When they arrived they found the place buzzing with quite a few visiting protectors and naturally, a whole company of dragons. Mrs T was a bit out of sorts after the long journey, as she was not a great flier. Her dragon, Tejas, was very gentle and getting on in dragon years. He flew very safely and steadily and always took great care of his protector, a sort of role reversal which amused the others enormously. Angus carried her bag and heard her tutting as she saw a familiar long black leather coat hanging from a peg just inside the castle entrance.

When they entered the Great Hall, Angus recognised some old faces he had not seen since the Trials. He was delighted to see Liam again, the young Irish lad who protected Gilmor, and Kadin the Emirati who partnered the Egyptian dragon Nehebkau, now living in Dubai. There were a few strangers there too, obviously new recruits. One was a city type in a sharp suit, terribly well spoken and introduced himself as Robert Fitch. He in turn seemed much taken with a striking young woman with long jet black hair. Both were deeply engrossed in conversation with Rathlin.

"Ah there you are dear. How was your flight?" said Rathlin as he greeted his wife warmly with a kiss.

"It was uneventful, just the way Tejas and I like it!" she replied curtly and frowned in the direction of the dark haired woman.

Ignoring this gesture, Rathlin turned to Angus.

"Angus, this is Miss Quinton-Jones... she's been looking forward to meeting you."

"How do you do Angus Munro, I am indeed delighted to meet you" said Miss Quinton-Jones.

"Pleased to meet you Miss..."

"Please call me Meredith!" she said as she extended an elegantly manicured hand with incredibly long painted fingernails.

She grasped Angus's hand firmly and shook it in a businesslike manner. Meredith had held his hand so strongly that the nails had left an indent where they touched his wrist. Although he thought she was a beautiful woman, she was also quite scary and he was not sure he liked her much. Her eyes were dark pools which seemed to analyse him with their intense glare, as if trying to penetrate his innermost thoughts.

After the new recruits had introduced themselves, Rathlin called the few assembled protectors to order and warned them of the potential threat of the wayward Felspar. His robust and powerful voice was punctuated by a faint tap-tapping noise. At first, Angus wondered where it came from, and then glancing around the room he saw the source of the distraction. Meredith Quinton-Jones was leaning on the large stone mantelpiece combing back her slick mane of hair with one hand while her other hand beat out a rhythm with her long fingernails. Mrs Tek shot an annoyed glance in her direction and Angus thought he was not the only one who had not taken to the new protector.

The briefing over and done with, Rathlin called Angus over to one side.

"How are you today lad?" he asked with a concerned look on his face.

"I'm okay" replied Angus matter-of-factly.

"Good… I want to show you something new we have set-up… follow me" said Rathlin.

The head of the SSDP led Angus across to the lighthouse and entered with a knock on the door. He motioned for Angus to sit at a laptop computer and at the press of a button the screen opened up a window. At first, all Angus could see was white static snow, like a television channel that is not tuned in properly, but then it began to disperse and a light bluish glow began to form. As the image cleared further, Angus recognised the location.

"It's Krubera… but how?" he asked.

"Courtesy of Miss Quinton-Jones" replied Rathlin, "She's been very helpful, although Aurora doesn't like her much!" Angus did not reply to that as Finian appeared on the screen with Godroi at his side.

"Good morning Angus… I see you've been introduced to our new toy" said the Ward.

"Hi Godroi… Finian… yes its brill… how did you know we were here?" asked Angus inquisitively.

"We have been reliably informed that a signal flashes and it automatically connects when a transmission arrives…" replied Godroi, "apparently it works!" he laughed.

"We have the same at this end" added Rathlin.

"Do you recall anything more about the strange dragon from your dream, Angus?" asked Godroi.

"No" he answered honestly.

"Not to worry but it would seem that you received a message or premonition of some kind and we should not take it lightly. However, you must concentrate on remembering every detail should it happen again" said the Ward.

"I will try" replied Angus.

"It seems to me that you are experiencing at lot of changes and not the normal transformations a lad your age would expect to go through" said Godroi. "All I can say is that you are not the only one affected by the Dragonore."

"What do you mean?" asked Angus, confused.

"Finian has some symptoms from exposure to the Dragonore and I recall from memory that this has happened before, though it is not common among humans" replied Godroi. "You must tell me of anything out of the ordinary that happens to you Angus, as you seem to be extremely susceptible to the energy of the Cor Stan, and the powers it induces!"

Angus was worried by this revelation but Godroi reassured him he was in no danger.

"You have nothing to fear Angus. If these powers develop they will only serve you well. You are very fortunate and unique, and especially worthy of this" he added mysteriously.

Chapter 8

'Gateposts'

Angus was daydreaming in his History class about his last trip to Calmor and all that had transpired during that week. After the Trials of the Cor Stan, he thought life would settle down and, he, and Pyrra would see out the weekends finding other hidden dragons. Never in his wildest dreams did he think his life could get so complicated. Angus looked up, feigning attentiveness to avoid the wrath of Miss Thomas. Despite Godroi's, and subsequently, Rathlin's assurance, he was fine and had nothing wrong with him; Angus felt the Ward was holding something back. Ward Barfoot had been particularly strange when they first met, almost as if he knew Angus and he had also called him by a strange name. He could not remember what it was, but Angus knew that somehow he had to understand what was happening to him.

Later that wet and dreary night, feeling too agitated to concentrate on his book he flopped on his bed and closed his eyes. The orange after-glow of the light bulb on the ceiling permeated the darkness behind his eyelids and his mind followed the blob around as it swam before his eyes like some sort of living aquatic creature. His imagination gave it life and he watched as its colours changed from orange to yellow to green. Then the blob of colour grew and changed to purple as it filled his vision. His eyes were still closed and he blinked to rid his sight of the image but to no avail. Now keeping his eyes closed tightly Angus could distinguish shapes emerging from the purple glare. He was flying with Pyrra as they swooped low along a rock strewn valley. Then two pillars appeared. His mind told him that the visions he had before were about to return and he felt a knot in his stomach. At the same time he heard Godroi tell him to pay attention. Suddenly there was another flash of purple light as they sped faster towards the pillars. He thought they would crash into the rocks directly in their path and fearing the high-speed impact he put his arms up to protect himself.

The purple light subsided and he lowered his arms. He recognised Marnham Church before him. Angus studied the scene as instructed. At first it all looked as it should but then little details became more apparent, there was the stained glass window, but it was different, not quite finished and no gargoyle on the roof either. The images blurred, then he was watching the fight again, but try as he might, he could not intervene in any way. Angus watched helplessly as the same sequence of events played onwards toward an end he already knew. As the deathblow came back to haunt him, he flinched.

Forcing himself back to consciousness he hit his head on the bedside cabinet as he rolled off the bed!

Cold water ran down Angus' face as the ice melted in the towel his Mum had placed on his head. He sat at the kitchen table and watched as she fussed about the cupboards looking for the first aid kit.

"It's okay Mum I don't need a bandage!" he pleaded.

"It's in here somewhere…" she said, "and you'll at least let me put some ointment on it to reduce the swelling… ah got it!" she finished brandishing the red box in triumphant fashion. In spite of his protests the cream was administered to the rather nasty-looking lump that had appeared almost before Angus picked himself up from his bedroom carpet. It stung a little and he screwed his face up at his reflection in the mirror once he finally escaped his Mother's clutches. Now he had to go back down to the living room and sit with his parents for a couple of hours as his Mum did not want him going to sleep so soon after the accident in case he was concussed.

The next day Angus awoke feeling most out of sorts and as soon as school was finished he jumped on his bike and rode off to find Pyrra.

"So the visions came back again last night and caused you to hit your head?" she enquired once they had rendezvoused at the trees.

"Well the head was just an accident as I fell out of bed, but the dream was as I said" he replied.

"No sign of the other dragon?"

"I don't think so… but you were there… and then I saw…" he trailed off unable to say it out loud.

"Do not worry about that Angus as I am sure it will not come to pass" she reassured.

"But it all seemed so real in parts… like it was meant to happen!" he replied.

"Perhaps we should report this to Krubera through Calmor… Can you call them?" she asked.

Angus agreed that calling Rathlin was the best they could do for now and they flew a short distance to a secluded phone box on the edge of the village.

Dialling the number for Calmor Angus stood with the heavy door of the old fashioned red phone box heaved open so that Pyrra could hear the conversation. Rathlin answered.

"Angus, what a nice surprise… All's well I hope?" he asked quickly.

"Yes everything is fine!" replied Angus quickly, "I just wanted to update Godroi on the dream… I saw it again last night!"

"Indeed... You'd better tell me all about it then" said Rathlin earnestly.

Angus told the same story as he had to Pyrra leaving out no detail. In fact Pyrra stood behind him saying 'and remember the...', 'and don't forget', so he was unlikely to miss anything anyway. Once he had finished Rathlin said nothing for a few seconds before finally answering.

"It seems to me we should be able to use this to help... I will call Godroi immediately and see if it jogs his memory" replied the head of the SSDP. "In the meantime I have a job for you, are you up for it?"

"Yeah, cool. What is it?" replied Angus eagerly.

"I need you to look in on a new dragon by the name of Caedmon. He is seeing out the Great Hibernation on the gatepost of a large country house in Wellshire..." said Rathlin as he proceeded to give Angus full instructions.

Ten minutes later Pyrra touched down near an old estate set in the picturesque countryside of Wellshire. It was a stately home surrounded by vast ornamental gardens, which in turn were flanked by thick woodland and all of it completely enclosed by a high dry stone wall, full of flints and typical of the area. Angus had seen all of this from the air because once on the ground all he could see was the thick stone wall and the dark trees towering behind it. According to Rathlin's instruction the main gate was where they would find the dragon, Caedmon.

"I think I met him at the Trials" said Pyrra as they walked along the country road to a large recess in the wall, set back from the roadside. "Quite an affable chap if I recall" she added. As they got nearer the wrought iron gateway, Angus could see not one, but two large stones on both of the end pillars. They were very striking with each dragon mirroring the other in a rampant pose, fore-claws raised ready to defend or attack.

Both dragons faced the approach to the gate as if they were guardians to a fortress.

"Which one is it Pyrra?" asked Angus.

"The left one is an empty shell... Caedmon, are you there?" she called up to the right hand statuette.

Nothing happened and no reply came from the dragon.

"Caedmon, my name is Pyrra and this is Angus from the SSDP, can you speak to us please?" she said politely and patiently.

"Why do you disturb my sleep?" was the stern reply from above.

Angus felt that the dragon was having a bad day. Either that or Pyrra had remembered the wrong dragon as this one was decidedly grumpy.

"Rathlin Tek sent us to speak to you... he said you had some information for us!" called up Angus, trying to help. Caedmon sprang from his perch on the gate and morphed to full size as he jumped to the ground. His dark grey skin reflected the trees that lightly swayed in the breeze; his body indicating hostility.

"Why can't you SDDP people just leave me alone?" he roared, "All I want is some peace and quiet... I've been here for 728 years and it would be nice to be allowed to sleep peacefully! I don't need protecting by busybodies!"

Angus and Pyrra exchanged puzzled glances.

"Rathlin told us you may have some information about Felspar!" asked Pyrra curtly.

"Felspar? Don't know any Felspar... now be off with you or..."

"Or you'll what?" growled Pyrra raising her body to its full height.

The grey dragon looked like he was about to rise to the challenge but then his eyes narrowed and he began to retreat slightly.

"I told you I don't know any Felspar and I certainly did not ask Rathlin Tek or anyone else for that matter to interfere in my hibernation..." he snarled, "Now if you'll excuse me!"

With that he turned his back and morphed back into the statuette on the gatepost.

Giving up on the task Rathlin had set them the friends took off for Piggleston. It was getting late and Angus had to get back for dinner and to complete his homework.

"I can't understand what was wrong with him" said Pyrra, "he is certainly not as I remember him."

"Maybe Rathlin got it wrong, but he did say that a protector had told him Caedmon had some information on Felspar, although the dragon was reluctant to get involved" added Angus.

"You're sure Rathlin said that Caedmon wanted to speak to us?"

"Totally!" replied Angus, "Caedmon was very specific to the protector that he would only speak to you!"

"Well, we will just need to take it up with Rathlin on Saturday" she said as they touched down in the wooded area near the sweet shop.

Angus unchained his bike and began to ride home.

"See you in a couple of days" he called out behind him, confusing an old lady walking her little Jack Russell dog, as she could see no-one else around. 'Strange kids nowadays' she said to her little dog as she watched the boy race out of sight.

Chapter 9

'Searching for Stones'

The rest of the week dragged for Angus, with the chores of schoolwork and Kleanware orders passing so slowly, he thought they would never end. He was slightly disappointed not to be visited by the dream dragon again. He still managed to visit Pyrra on Friday afternoon to make sure she was okay and eventually both friends were on their way to Calmor Castle in the Irish Sea.

Angus could see Rathlin as he walked from the lighthouse to the castle and he waved when the ponytailed man saw them approach for a landing.

"So how did it go with Caedmon then?" Rathlin asked, greeting his guests.

"Not too well I'm afraid" replied Pyrra.

"Really?" said Rathlin, surprised. "How so?"

"He made it plain that he had not spoken to anyone nor had he asked to be visited… In fact he was extremely rude!" replied

Pyrra indignantly.

"That's strange, as Tom was very clear about the message… perhaps you got the wrong dragon… so you learned nothing more of Felspar then?" asked Rathlin.

"No, we didn't" replied Angus shrugging his shoulders.

"Well never mind, let's go inside and find the others as we have some work to do" said Rathlin, gesturing towards the castle.

Mrs T was sitting on one of the large sofas in the Great Hall when Angus entered. She was talking to Liam and Kadin who both peered at her notebook as she pointed to various names.

"I see you are already briefing the boys on their task" said Rathlin jovially to his wife as he strode towards the fireplace.

"Not at all, I thought I would leave that to you… I was just giving them a sample of the fantastic history Angus and I uncovered" she replied

"Jolly good… it will save me time with explanations" smiled Rathlin.

"What's going on Rathlin?" asked Angus.

"Aurora my love, have you managed to whittle that list down a little more?" he asked.

"I've tried Rathlin, but it's difficult to know what to look for."

"I have complete confidence in you my dear" he said

smiling at his wife. "Why don't you go through them?" he urged. Mrs T began to run through the list of potential portals, giving a concise reason for choosing each one.

"Excellent work" said the head of the SSDP as she reached the end. "I visited some of the sites last week, but alas there are far too many for Cyru and I to cover alone and that is where you come in" he explained.
The three lads perked up at the thought of an SSDP task, especially one that involved flying on a dragon.

"We will split up into pairs" he continued, "Liam, Kadin, you two check out Drumskinny, Goatstones and Castlerigg… Angus and I will take Bryn Celli Ddu and Cairnholy… We should be able to manage that in a day."

"I take it you'll be having map locations?" smiled Liam. "Although Drumskinny is one I know… hey Kadin I can show you where I come from and maybe introduce you to me Mam, that'll be grand" he said to Kadin who looked confused but nodded politely anyway.

"I've marked up a copy for you and some directions just in case you need them" replied Aurora Tek handing him his notes.

"What is this Goatstones anyway?" asked Liam brightly. Angus told him what he could remember from his research in the library, as he had liked the sound of this one.

"They belong to a class of monument known as a Four-Poster Stone Circle and are mainly found in Scotland… particularly in Perthshire, but this one is in Northumberland…" Angus began in reply, before being stopped by Liam.

"Okay Angus, spare us the history lesson!" the boy laughed. "I guess it's up north somewhere… I know, follow the map…" he said winking at Mrs T, "and Castlerigg is in the Lake District… it looks like an eyeball from the sky… sure that'll be easy to spot then!" he smiled. "Come on then Kadin lets find some dragons… Race you back here then!" he called as he began to walk away. "Oh… by the way, what are we looking for?"

"We don't know… Just report anything unusual" said Rathlin with a shrug.

Angus felt he had something to add to this, but the words would not come to him. As they watched the two lads run excitedly to find their dragon partners, Rathlin turned to Angus.

"Well lad, are you ready to go?"

"Sure!" replied Angus looking thoughtful.

"Good. Let's rustle up Pyrra and Cyru and we'll be on our way… We'll be back by tea time" he called rather optimistically to his wife.

Rathlin tacked up Cyru, who was not in a good mood. He preferred to laze around at Calmor in the Blue Dragon Fire and the thought of flying around the country did not appeal to him. However the blue dragon consoled himself with the thought of stopping Felspar, should they be successful.

Pyrra tried to lighten Cyru's mood as they took off from the Island.

"Cheer up you... we might manage to find a football game to watch!" she bellowed as they slipped into dragon time to speed up the journey to Wales. Their destination was the Isle of Anglesey at the north-western extremity of Wales. Angus watched for a narrow stretch of water known as the Menai Strait which separated the isle from the mainland. A causeway spanned the gap and Angus figured it should be easy to spot from the air.

Soon the island was in sight and although much larger than Calmor they quickly located the megalith thanks to Mrs T's concise instructions. What surprised everyone was that there were two monuments at Bryn Celli Ddu, one built on top of the other. The first monument was a henge that contained a central stone circle and Angus could see this was almost completely covered by the chamber and cairn of the second monument.

"Magnificent!" was all Rathlin could say.

This was a significant prehistoric site and Rathlin was excited about it. Angus felt sure this was not the right place, even though it did have a mystical aura about it. He was not the only one to share the belief that the site was special. There were people in colourful flowing robes conducting some sort of ceremony, and remaining invisible, Rathlin and Angus crept closer and watched with great interest. Candles were placed in a circle, leaving a small opening through which to enter. The enclosed space was large enough to hold several people and a man and a woman stood in the centre with many others around them.

"It's some sort of wedding" whispered Rathlin.

The betrothed pair and their witnesses stood in the centre for the ceremony. A flat stone seemed to hold a special importance in the middle. At each end of the stone stood a vase holding a single flower and next to each flower was a crystal. Angus could see two candles had been placed between the vases and the man and woman lit these altar candles, before they continued to light the half circle of candles on their own sides. They met at the entrance to the circle and entered together, then took their place one at each end of the flat stone.

Rathlin and Angus stood silently mesmerised by the

ceremony. Even Pyrra and Cyru seemed entranced by it all. As usual for Angus, there was too much talking and some poems followed before the couple blew out, first, their own candles and then those in their half of the circle. They left the circle together, united by their pledges of love in the autumn sunshine. Angus was fascinated by the simple ceremony and wondered if Rathlin was thinking of his recent wedding to Aurora last April. His face was unreadable and eventually the wedding party drifted away to continue their festivities elsewhere.

When the site was quite empty, Rathlin, Angus and the dragons walked forward to explore. Silently, they studied a big stone, which was decorated with carvings on both sides.

"I think this is meant to stand upright" said Rathlin. The decorations consisted of long thin lines which passed over the top of the stone from each side. The carvings on one side had a kind of maze appearance incorporating a spiral, while the other side looked more like a zigzag pattern. Flowers adorned the big stone, presumably left over from the wedding.

"Do you think this is the place we're looking for?" asked Angus as he traced the grooves of the ancient stones artwork with his finger.

"I don't think it is Angus... What about you Pyrra?" said

Rathlin as he shook his head.

Pyrra did not recognise any of the carved symbols either, and they were nothing like the ones at Calmor. They all felt a bit deflated and Cyru slumped against a recumbent stone. He was totally disinterested in the whole project.

"Right then, we can tick that one off the list" he said sourly.

"Come on Cyru, we need to head north to Galloway" urged Rathlin.

Cyru brightened at the idea of leaving, and he led the way.

Angus watched in fascination as the isle passed below them. Pyrra and Cyru circled each other through the clouds enjoying the flight as they winged their way to Scotland over the sea and past the Isle of Man. 'I wonder how the others are getting on?' mused Angus to himself hoping that he and Rathlin would be the ones to find the portal. Soon they circled the Wigtown Bay in Galloway and saw the distinctive facade of the famous Cairnholy megalith fanning out below them as they neared Kirkdale. Flying nearer they saw the individual stones, standing in an impressive line like soldiers on parade. Angus thought it looked like a row of teeth in a massive jaw and was amazed to think that this was five thousand years old!

"What do we know about Cairnholy?" Rathlin shouted back to Angus as they landed.

"Mrs T said that the name probably comes from Gaelic carn ulaidh which means treasure cairn... the stones were once banked up with a mound but the earth was removed some time later" he read from the notes she had given him.

Rathlin liked the look of the place and they explored the site keenly, but once again the stones indicated nothing out of the ordinary and he got the feeling that this was not the portal they were seeking.

By this time Cyru was positively sulking and seemed almost teenager-like in his resignation to what he considered yet another wasted journey. He was keen to get home and see if any of his friends had turned up at Calmor. A quick call to Mrs T confirmed that nothing had been found by Liam and Kadin at the other sites and they were already on their way back. Angus imagined they would soon be tucking into Dermot's flapjacks back at the castle.

"I bet Nehebkau and Gilmor are already in my favourite Blue Dragon Fire patch!" moaned Cyru.

"What now?" Angus asked.

"Well it seems a shame to come this far for nothing... how about a change of tasks?" replied Rathlin mysteriously.

"Like what?" Angus asked, intrigued.

"I believe that there may be a dragon hibernating in Dundee

and it seems a shame to be this far north and not have a look. What do you think?" replied Rathlin.

"Sounds cool... I'm in... what about you Pyrra?" said Angus turning to the green dragon.

"Let's go!" she said smiling.

"Oh that's nice... no one ever asks me what I want!" whinged Cyru causing Rathlin to shake his head in exasperation.

An irritated Rathlin took to the sky with a defiant dragon and even Pyrra looked a bit weary. Angus reflected on the day's disappointments and discoveries as they set off for Dundee.

Chapter 10

'Twa Hame's'

Angus marvelled at the scenery below him as the quartet made their way northeast towards Dundee. No one was speaking to each other. It was not long before two large cities appeared sprawling along the horizon, one on the left and one on the right.

"Glasgow and Edinburgh!" shouted Rathlin pointing first to the left and then the right as he recognised Angus' quizzical look.

They pushed on between the two, veering more towards Edinburgh on the right side. Angus drank in the stunning view of Edinburgh Castle sitting atop its fortified position in the heart of the Scottish capital. Rathlin waved and indicated for Pyrra to follow Cyru and he leant forward to speak to his sulking dragon, they switched to normal time and dove towards two bridges spanning the estuary near the city.

"WOOHOO!" shouted Angus as they sped under the road bridge and over the old but solid-looking railway bridge at the same time as a train passed over it.

If the people in the cars or the train had Dragonore they would have been astonished at the sight of two dragons and their riders acrobatically swooping and diving around the bridges. All

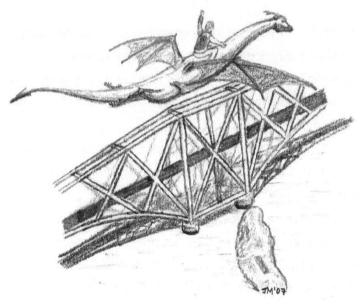

too soon, the fun had to end and the two dragons were brought back on track and into dragon time. They followed a motorway that ran parallel to a railway line running northwards, and passed over a loch. The exhilaration of their acrobatics at the bridges had finally put a smile on Cyru's face.

The countryside became steeper and rose as they progressed. Rathlin indicated Angus and Pyrra to follow him and they veered left towards two peaks split by the motorway.

The cars slowly crawled along the tarmac road and the dragons, still in dragon time, swept through the gap just above the cars. Angus gasped as the hidden valley behind the summits opened up before him to reveal a river with rolling hills rising up in the background. The road spilled from the opening in the hillside and onto a long curving bridge that swept away to the right. All four travellers whooped as they sped past the left side of the bridge and swung under it to follow the river eastwards.

Angus began to wonder how much further it would be to Dundee when Rathlin pointed to the horizon. At first Angus could not make out much apart from a large hillside with a radio mast and a monument on it, a few high rise flats and the odd tower of a church but as they swept closer he began to distinguish more detail. Like Edinburgh, Dundee had two bridges although much smaller in height, but each took the same type of traffic and Angus watched the cars as they barely moved along its length. Rathlin must have signalled to Pyrra because the young protector's eyes blurred as she changed back into normal time, the cars appearing to speed-up. He looked down and saw a large sailing ship moored near the bridges with its tall masts standing proud, adorned with signalling flags that billowed in the wind. He followed Rathlin down as they swung away from the ship and towards the grey stone buildings that formed the heart of the city. They turned a few corners sweeping between the grey buildings and Pyrra stayed as close to Cyru as possible. People below went about their usual Saturday shopping, totally unaware of the unusual aerial visitors. Cyru pulled up abruptly. They had flown into a busy pedestrian precinct and he hovered looking for a suitable place to land. Eventually Rathlin pointed to an alleyway and the blue dragon flapped his wings powerfully to gain height, blowing several of the shoppers sideways. Pyrra followed him over the building and Angus watched, amused, as several Dundonians look up, confused by the sudden gust of wind that had nearly knocked them off their feet.

The dragons landed at the back of the building and both the protectors slipped quickly off their dragons hoping they had not been seen.

"You two better stay up high out of the way" said Rathlin, "Okay Angus, this way I think" he added indicating the alleyway.

"So how do you know you're way about?" Angus asked trying to keep up with Rathlin's long stride.

"Oh I've been here before… although it's changed a little from my last visit" he replied looking at an odd pair of bronze states. "It's a nice city… and did you notice the large hill?"

"Yeah… but no castle on it like Edinburgh" replied Angus.

"Well spotted… but both are extinct volcanoes!" said Rathlin.

"Cool!" replied the young protector as he began to edge toward the two statues.

Angus could not resist a look and he walked around them smiling at the detail in the bronze sculptures. He had seen the characters before in a comic book but he could only recall the name of the smaller statue and her name was Minnie the Minx.

"Get a move on Angus!" called Rathlin.

Angus ran after the head of the SSDP and as they strode a little further through the pedestrian precinct, he spotted the largest dragon statue he had ever seen.

"No way!" he shouted before running up to stroke its head. The bronze statue was tinged green due to its exposure to the elements and it depicted a dragon with its head sitting low to the ground and its tail wrapped and curled around a vertical flagpole.

"Is this what you came to see?" he said to Rathlin.

"Absolutely, but it seems my deduction from the notes a dragon would be hibernating here, were wrong" he replied looking at his Dragonore which stayed cold.

Angus pulled the pouch that held his Dragonore from under his jacket and t-shirt and removed the precious stone to inspect it. Sure enough the small rock stayed cool indicating that no dragon was present. The young protector walked to the other side of the statue to take in the superb detail the sculpture had managed to etch into the bronze. As he did so the Dragonore warmed almost imperceptibly.

"Rathlin come over here a second" he said excitedly.

"What is it?" enquired Rathlin.

"Take out your Dragonore and tell me what you think" replied Angus.

"By Jove it's slightly warm… but how?" he asked.

"It could be our dragons but I suppose another dragon might be nearby" said Angus hopefully.

"I'll tell you what… why don't we split up and fly low over the city" said Rathlin, "we've come all this way and it would be a shame to miss a dragon for the want of a ten minute search."

They agreed on a bearing and soon both protectors were in the air flying in opposite directions, Angus to the east and Rathlin to the west. The whole city lay before Angus and he took in the sights and smells that drifted up towards them. They passed over a church and soon came upon not one but what appeared to be two football stadiums, right next to each other. Angus was just taking this in when he realised his Dragonore was glowing brightly.

"Pyrra do you feel that?" he called forward.

"Yes it's just back there" she replied as she banked left to return the way they had come.

As they flew over the church again Angus noticed the steeple had a weathervane on it and he laughed as he recognised its shape.

"It's there Pyrra… lets land" he said pointing into the church yard.

The green dragon touched down on the grass lawn and Angus leapt from her back before she had even managed to fold her wings. He ran to the end of the building as he tried to get the best possible view of the weathervane.

"Over here Pyrra!" he shouted back to her.

"Hold your horses Angus… I'm coming" she laughed.

When she caught him up Pyrra looked upwards.

"Well, do you want to do the honours?" she asked.

Angus remembered the first time he had asked a dragon to come out of hiding and he was sure he could do much better now.

"Hello up there…" he bellowed, "we're from The Secret Society of Dragon Protectors. Can you come down please?"

"Very subtle…" said Pyrra winking at Angus and then

looking up, "but seemingly effective."

Angus followed her gaze and could see a morphing dragon as it emerged from the weathervane. The dragon was light blue like Cyru but not quite the same shade and as it landed deftly beside them he could see it was a female by the size of her head.

"Whit's aw this noise aboot?" she said sternly, "And who are ya tae waken me up?"

Pyrra looked perplexed and turned her head to Angus.

"Well you woke her up, but I'm not sure what was said… so?" she urged cocking her head towards the dragon to indicate that Angus had the lead.

"Hi I'm Angus and this is Pyrra… we're from the SSDP and we've come to find you and help protect you" he replied.

At first the dragon just looked from Angus to Pyrra and back again, her face showing no emotion at all and Angus was beginning to wonder if she understood him.

"Well now why didn't ya just say so in the first place!" she replied in a broad Scottish accent but, as far as Angus could remember, not as broad as Nathair the Wyrm. "Ma name is Cairistiona an am pleased tae meet ya" she finished smiling.

"We're pleased to meet you as well… we came with some friends, Cyru, a dragon, and Rathlin Tek, the head of the

SSDP" said Angus.

"Well am very honoured to have such noble visitors" replied the blue dragon. "Where are these others you speak of?"

"We split up while we were looking for you" replied Angus. "Pyrra can you go and get them?"

"Of course I can" she replied having only really picked up some of the conversation.

As Pyrra took off to hunt for Cyru, Angus decided he should get to know the new dragon.

"How long have you been hibernating here?" he asked.

"Oh a few hundred years or so, but a woke recently due to some strange dream ah was havin!" she replied.

"I know all about that... a bright blue light and an unknown old dragon" said Angus.

"That's right!" replied the dragon incredulously. "You really must be a good protector!"

Angus blushed and quickly changed the subject.

"Listen Cairistiona, I know about another dragon that used to hibernate in a weathervane..." he paused, not sure how to approach such a delicate subject, as he knew dragons tended to get attached to their hiding places, "well... it kind of died."

"Really... How?" asked the dragon inquisitively.

"He was struck by lightning!"

"Nice! How many times coz av been struck ten times?" Cairistiona replied proudly.

"I… don't think your getting me… he was eventually killed by lightning after being hit many times… just like you" explained Angus, hoping she would catch on.

"Really… imagine that!" she replied apparently surprised.

"Wouldn't it be safer if you found a new hiding place?" he asked patiently.

"Well a suppose so, but am a bit reluctant tae leave here" she replied, "Ya see av discovered they play fitbaw nearby and av grown quite accustomed tae watchin it!" she explained. Angus thought about her answer as it sounded very like another dragon he knew; obviously they had an awful lot more in common than just their blue scales.

"So why don't you hide in the dragon statue in the high street?" he suggested.

"Whit dragon statue is this?" she asked.

"There's a brilliant bronze dragon statue in the high street…" he replied, "just over that way!" he finished pointing in the general direction he and Pyrra had first come from.

"Well now would ya credit that!" replied Cairistiona. "C'mon jump on then and let's have a look!" she said bending her neck and shoulders to make it easy for him to climb on her back.

111

"We should wait for the others…"

"Nonsense!" she cut in, "they will catch us up!" and with that said she leapt into the air with Angus scrabbling to stay on.

Angus managed to keep a grip on the impulsive blue dragon's neck whilst scanning the skies for any sign of the others. His search was cut short as the dragon began to dive for the Dundee high street and he was convinced that she was about to land on the shoppers swarming below. The bronze dragon was clearly visible and Cairistiona swung over it, narrowly avoiding the flag pole that formed part of the statue and then settled directly upon its back. Angus stared incredulously as passers by went within inches of the blue dragon's wings without even knowing it. He also knew that as long as he stayed on her back, he, like her, would also remain invisible.

"Tae think this was here and a didna know it!" cried the excited dragon.

"So will you hide here now?" asked Angus.

"Nae problem this will be a great place and I can also see when the humans are going tae the fitbaw!" she replied.

"What's so good about that?" asked Angus perplexed.

"Well, seeing as it's nearly time fur kick-off I can show ya!" replied the blue dragon as she flicked out her wings and flapped for height, blowing the hats and scarves off some football supporters walking to the stadium.

For a second time, Angus found himself clinging round the dragon's neck. Clearly Cairistiona was not used to carrying passengers. He really wished the others would get back and yet again he looked around hoping to spot them but saw only rooftops and empty sky. They began to drift down, and Angus sat up as the two football stadiums appeared, as before, right next to each other. One was blue roofed with dark blue seats and the other was white roofed with orange coloured seats. The football fans were queued up outside the orange stadium and as Cairistiona landed on top of one of the stands, Angus could see that the teams were out, warming up on the pitch.

"A love it here, the atmosphere is great…" explained the feisty female, "the noise, excitement… and the pehs!"

"Pehs?" asked Angus totally confused and thinking this dragon was definitely mad.

"Aye… Pehs… yi know… mince meat pehs?" she elaborated.

"Oh right… pies! Do you like them?" he asked.

"A love em!" she replied licking her lips in a comical fashion, "Very tasty!"

Angus laughed at her and watched as the players finished

warming up and began to make their way back to the dressing rooms. Parts of the crowd cheered or jeered depending on which team's player passed them.

"So this is where you got to?" said the voice of Pyrra suddenly.

Angus spun around so quickly he almost lost his footing on the roof but caught himself quickly.

"Oh... Hi... glad you managed to find us okay" he replied.

"Well it was not hard for us to spot a blue dragon sitting on top of a white roof" laughed Rathlin.

Cyru stood behind Pyrra almost hiding as introductions to the new dragon were made. Angus literally had to drag him towards Cairistiona when it was his turn to be introduced. It was the first time Angus had ever seen him quiet and he did not realise the dragon was shy.

The new dragon explained about her home and how she got there. She also explained that Angus had shown her the high street hiding place and that she would live there from now on.

"So how did you get to be here?" Rathlin asked.

"Well that's a long story... I had my ancestors in this region but one of them brought shame to the family" she replied.

"Really... How so?" enquired Rathlin further.

"It really is shameful... my great uncle... he ate humans ya see!" she said lowering her head.

"Wow, did he really eat people?" exclaimed Angus.

"It is not very honourable Angus and something most dragons will not do, but there is always one or two that give the rest of us a bad name" said Pyrra sadly.

"Aye there is... Ya see he waited at a well one day and ate a maiden that came to get water... then her sister came to find her and he ate her as well!"

"That's a very sad story" said Rathlin.

"Oh it disnae end there... Ya see there were nine sisters in aw, and the daft father sent one after the other until he ran oot o daughters" added the blue dragon sadly.

"Oh my!" said Rathlin astonished.

"Anyway the father eventually came tae find them and when he saw whit had happened he rounded up the villagers" she shook her head, "Well I dinnae need tae tell ya whit happened tae ma uncle next!"

Her dreadful story fascinated Angus who thought he would find out more when he got the chance but for now he was content to watch the football as the players re-emerged to great applause and cheering.

The trip to Dundee had more than made up for the

disappointment of not finding the portal and he hoped they would have better luck tomorrow. For now, he was content and Angus was also enjoying the sight of Cyru inching closer to the edge of the roof to watch the game, while he also tried to look at Cairistiona without being caught. Pyrra just shook her head in amusement and spoke to the newly found dragon as Rathlin listened in. Cyru eventually plucked up the courage to speak to Cairistiona nearer half time and when he found out she liked pies he disappeared. Rathlin had just started to get worried about his young dragon when Cyru returned with five pies he had somehow acquired.

"Eat them while their hot!" he said to Pyrra.

It turned out she and Rathlin did not want one, so the two blue dragons ate one extra each, and forgetting his shyness, Cyru started to talk animatedly while he explained the rules of football to the newly found dragon.

When the game had finished, the three dragons and two passengers flew once more towards the back of the high street.

"Well I must thank ya for finding me and making me realise I wisnae alone, an fur ma new hame" said Cairistiona atop the building they had landed on.

"We will be back to try and find a protector for you" replied Rathlin.

"Yeah and I will show you the way to Calmor!" added Cyru excitedly.

"Aye a would like that, an yi can come visit me here now a have twa hames like the fitbaw!" she smiled.

The protectors waved goodbye as Pyrra and Cyru headed for Calmor. Angus watched the newest and, as it turned out, youngest dragon morph into her new home.

Chapter 11

'Caedmon'

Rathlin and Angus walked wearily into the Great Hall of Calmor Castle, whilst Pyrra and Cyru elected to stay outside and laze in the Blue Dragon Fire, watching the sun go down. It had been a long but eventful day and both protectors looked forward to relaxing on the soft settee by the fireplace drinking a warm cup of something and eating flapjacks.

"Aurora dear, are you here?" shouted Rathlin as they flopped down on the couches.

"I'm just in the kitchen… would you like something to drink?" she called.

"Oh yes please… I would love a cup of tea… you're a star!" he replied enthusiastically. "What about you Angus?"

"Hot chocolate would be great thanks!" replied Angus as he sank back into the cushions.

Mrs T placed a tray on the low square table that sat between the two sofas; it had three large mugs on it and a plate of Dermot's flapjacks.

"So, did you find it then?" asked Aurora looking at Rathlin. Rathlin took a long slurp of his tea savouring the taste before he answered.

"Alas no… the two sites we visited were fabulous but not what we were looking for… one of them even had a wedding being conducted in it!" he replied.

"Really… I would like to hear about that!" she said with interest. "What about the trip to Dundee, was it as fruitful as the cake?" she laughed at her own joke.

"Very much" he replied in-between sips, "In fact I think we might see a lot of the young dragon we found."
While Angus silently sipped his hot chocolate and demolished the plate of biscuits, Rathlin explained all about Cairistiona.

"Well, that is certainly an interesting development. We shall have to keep an eye on Cyru" she said thoughtfully, "So who won the game of football?"
Rathlin looked perplexed as he had not really watched the game but Angus knew.

"Dundee United!" replied Angus as he finished off the last flapjack.

"Angus Munro! You will never eat your dinner young man!" she scolded standing up to clear the tray.
Mrs T walked to the passage that led to the kitchen and stopped.

"Oh by the way, I called your Mother, Angus, to assure her you were fine and had arrived okay… she seemed very busy but was glad you're safe" she said turning to the boy.

"Thanks Mrs T… What's for dinner?" he grinned.

"It's a surprise" she smiled back, "I can't believe you're still hungry after eating all those biscuits!"

"He's a growing lad!" laughed Rathlin. "Now let's go and get cleaned up for dinner and check on the dragons!"

Dinner for Angus was over in seconds and he made his excuses to the Tek's before running off to the lower cavern where the dragon sanctuary was. He wanted to go down and see who was visiting but he already knew from Mrs T that Liam and Kadin had left already. Kadin had to get home for school on Sunday morning which Angus found difficult to understand, it seemed they had different weekends in the Middle East. He would like to go visit Kadin in Dubai one day as it sounded quite an interesting place. While he had been thinking about his Emirati friend, Angus had gone through the secret doorway in the Great Hall, down into the cellar and used his Dragonore to open the door with no handle. He switched on the new lighting that Rathlin had installed in the tunnel and ran down to the boat landing area below, before he made his way to the great cavern that housed the dragons.

When Angus reached the cavern he could not find Pyrra where they had arranged to meet, but he did not have long to wait as the sound of flapping wings approached from the direction of the boat landing area. Angus turned to see Pyrra and Cyru flying down the passageway towards the centre of the cavern where he stood. Then he saw something else. It was Caedmon and he was right behind the two dragons, eyes fixed firmly on their exposed flanks. Angus ran towards Pyrra shouting.

"Look out Pyrra, it's Caedmon and he's going to attack!" he yelled.

Pyrra either did not hear him, or she did not understand, but the green dragon just casually flew towards him and landed in front of him, apparently unconcerned.

"Pyrra what's going on?" asked Angus confused as Cyru and then Caedmon landed deftly beside her.

"Angus, meet Caedmon… he's just arrived and we've been having an interesting conversation outside…" she replied. "He is a bit confused about our last meeting."

Angus was still very mystified by what was happening and even more so when Caedmon spoke.

"Angus Munro… so pleased to meet you… I've heard all about you and was fortunate to meet Pyrra at Krubera but I'm sorry to say I did not get the chance to meet you" said the grey dragon with great eloquence.

Angus was stunned by what he had just heard and he looked to Pyrra for some clue but she stayed straight faced giving him no indication that this was any sort of joke. He decided to play along.

"But we met you a few days ago… Don't you remember?" he asked seriously.

"Did you? I'm sure I would have remembered that" replied the grey dragon looking very puzzled, "Pyrra told me the same thing but I really don't think we've met… perhaps my memory is worse than I thought!" he finished.

"Well you certainly seem a different dragon from the one at our last meeting but I'm sure it was you!" replied Angus in exasperation.

"Caedmon, why don't you tell Angus why you've come?" said Pyrra enjoying the game.

"Of course, what was I thinking? Felspar paid me a surprise visit recently. That's why I asked to see Pyrra. I knew that only she and the legendary Angus Munro could deal with this!" he replied enthusiastically and seeing his now captive audience were eager to hear more, Caedmon continued to explain. "He sought me out where I was hibernating… He wanted to know about Godroi."

"What did he ask you?" asked Angus urgently realising that

this really was important.

"Oh nothing really, just some questions about Godroi's hiding place during the Great Hibernation... Well I told him it was no great secret that he had used the stained glass window in Marnham Church the whole time... Mine is a fabulous hiding place as well and a very important human lives there, some heiress who inherited Quinton Lodge... I see her sometimes when she drives her very fast red car... scares me half to death every time she screeches down the gravel drive... Well imagine my surprise when she joined the SSDP and turned up at Calmor recently!" he went on.

"What else did Felspar ask you?" said Pyrra with great subtlety as she tried to steer the conversation back to the dragon's visit.

Caedmon loved a receptive audience and took great delight in recounting the rest of the story of his meeting with the black dragon to Angus, Pyrra and Cyru. The grey dragon was so wrapped up in listening to his own voice that he did not seem to notice the pair growing more and more anxious as he repeated the whole conversation practically word for word. Angus almost laughed out loud when he glanced at Cyru; the blue dragon looked at Caedmon with an extremely vacant expression on his scaly face.

"Of course, I told him, I remembered the location quite easily… young Godroi hiding in that stained glass window at St Georges Church at Marnham, just as soon as the glazier had finished and almost before it was installed… a bit of a joke it was really…" droned on the grey dragon.

"SAY THAT AGAIN?" shouted Angus suddenly and causing Cyru to snap out of his stupor.

"What! Well I was just saying that Felspar came to…"

"No not that bit… about the window!" pushed Angus.

"Oh… well, it was just about finished but Godroi could not wait and was already using it before it was fully complete and…"

"That's it!" exclaimed Angus.

"What is it Angus?" asked Pyrra sensing her exceptional young protector was onto something.

Angus ignored her question for now and pushed Caedmon for answers.

"What did you and Felspar talk about after the window?" he asked incisively.

"Ah now let me see… yes… it was about George the knight and how he was depicted in the painting as defeating the dragon… well we all know the truth eh, don't we?" replied the grey dragon jovially, enjoying the telling of the story and unaware of Angus' urgency, "Of course this was early on… before Argent pitched up to torment him… I say, weren't you and he a bit of an item?" he asked suddenly turning to Pyrra.

"I think at the time you are talking about, Argent and I were off on a journey, trying to find me a safe hiding place" she replied directing her answer at Angus.

He at once understood the implications. Pyrra and Argent were not with Godroi during the time that Felspar was trying to pinpoint in history. Angus now knew that the black dragon was planning to attack Godroi before he became Ward, when even his friends were not around to help him. It sounded like pure fantasy but it all made sense to him, now all he had to do was convince the others. Angus still could not get his head around the possibility of time travel, or how it could be achieved. He felt sure the dream he had experienced on two occasions, full of purple flashes and blinding light, held the answer. They both had a common theme and he just needed to find out what it meant.

Angus and Pyrra made their excuses and took leave of Caedmon and Cyru; the blue dragon looking forlorn at being left with the visitor. The pair went up to the castle to consult with Rathlin and told him the news.

"Well I never…" he replied after their concise version of the events, whittled down from what Caedmon had told them. "So you really think Felspar is a threat?" he asked them.

"I know he is!" replied Angus assuredly, "It's going to happen... I just don't know when!"

"Aurora can you sift through these possible portal sites and we can check them out tomorrow" he asked his wife. "We need to speak to Godroi at once young man and explain what is going on... hopefully there is something we can do to put an end to this nonsense!"

Chapter 12

'Volunteered'

Angus ran to keep up with Rathlin as the SSDP head strode purposefully in the direction of the lighthouse. Pyrra flew on ahead and he wished he had hitched a ride with her. It was dark and Angus watched the revolving light spin its warning into the darkness. The only sound he could hear was the sea as it lashed the rocks around the island, and his own breath. Before they reached Dermot's lodgings the warden called to them from the dog pen as he had just come back from walking them down on the beach.

"Well now sir… what would be bringing you down here at this time of night?" he asked.

"Sorry Dermot, it couldn't wait I'm afraid… we really need to speak to Godroi urgently… do you mind?" replied Rathlin at once.

"Of course… go right in… I'll be putting the kettle on once I'm finished with the dogs" replied Dermot.

Having been brought up to speed by Angus, the Head of the SSDP knew that he must get in touch with Finian immediately to warn him about the planned revenge. The young protector, although headstrong at times, always seemed to be caught up in the middle of things and during the short time Rathlin had known the lad, one thing was sure; Angus had a special talent. It was as yet untapped and certainly had not shown its full potential, but it was there and he was not the only one who believed it. Angus had convinced him Felspar was planning to do something destructive to the SSDP and he was not about to let it happen without a fight. He was extremely agitated and knew they must act quickly as he sat down and switched on the satellite link donated by Meredith Quinton-Jones to celebrate her acceptance into the SSDP.

The familiar face of Finlan appeared on the screen before them with his hood down. Angus was still amazed by this piece of technology and found the whole thing very cool.

"It's totally James Bond!" he laughed.

Ward Godroi appeared on the screen beside The Watcher and listened solemnly as Angus and Rathlin explained what they had discovered.

"It is true I was quite alone at that time… I was very impetuous in those days and could not wait until they had completed the windows fully" said the Ward.

"Do you recall the exact time?" asked Rathlin.

"It was June because I remember the summer solstice was celebrated the day after I moved into my window… the church took fourteen years to build and I took up residence in the year it was finished... now when was it 1237 or 1238?" he said to himself, "Mmmm let me think now... 1238!" he replied nodding.

"You're sure?" asked Rathlin seriously.

"I believe so... it's a little fuzzy but... yes I'm sure" replied the Ward smiling.

"How long was it before Argent joined you?" asked Angus.

"They did not put the gargoyles up for a few weeks after the window was installed, and he arrived after that" replied Godroi thoughtfully.

"So what do we do now?" asked Angus uncertainly.

"It seems that Felspar has somehow summoned the ancient power we dragons once held and thought gone... to be able to travel through time!" replied the golden dragon. "But all is not lost... we know what he is attempting to do and as yet he has not managed to do it. We must track him down and stop him before he finds the portal and uses it!"

"And what if we're too late?" questioned Angus doubtfully.

"Then there will be nothing else for it, Angus... You will have to follow him!" replied the Ward dramatically.

"ME?" replied Angus shocked, "But why me... What can I do against Felspar?"

"It will be up to you to secure the future of all dragons and preserve the true course of history, but you will not be alone as Pyrra will be there to help you!" reassured Godroi smiling.

Angus stood beside Rathlin looking at the screen. He could not believe what he had just heard and wanted to speak to Pyrra about it as soon as possible.

"Don't worry Angus we'll catch him before he travels back and you won't need to go anywhere!" comforted Rathlin.

"I hope so…" replied Angus but then he trailed off not knowing what else to say.

Rathlin switched the computer off after saying farewell to Finian and Godroi. Angus walked out of the Lighthouse in a daze and saw the welcome sight of Pyrra coming back towards them with Cyru trailing forlornly behind her.

"Well at least we have Godroi's information… That at least narrows it down a bit, but I will have to get Aurora working on the exact dates… we don't want to make a mistake just in case we need to use it" said Rathlin as they walked to meet the dragons.

Angus' head swam with the thought of what might happen. 'Even if he could travel back in time with Pyrra, how would he be able to stop Felspar?' The green dragon walked up to Angus and looked at her young protector's face.

"What's wrong?" she asked immediately concerned.

"Wait til you hear this…" he replied.

Chapter 13

'Faulty Dragonore'

Angus reached the castle without having the chance to discuss with Pyrra his reservations from the conversation with Ward Godroi. He only had time to explain what Godroi had asked them do, if required. Angus had not wished to admit to anyone but her, that the thought of pursuing Felspar scared him. Angus remembered how close Felspar had come to killing Pyrra on the last day of the Trials and he feared for her safety, if they proved to be no match for the dragon whose heart was as black as his skin. He prayed that they would be able to stop the rogue dragon before it was too late.

When they walked into the hall, Mrs T was hard at work as she laboured through her extensive notes. She barely glanced up intent on completing her filtering task by selecting only the remaining sites that matched the criteria described in Finian's notes.

It was getting late and she knew time was of the essence.

"I'm almost done Rathlin..." she said absentmindedly with her pen poised on the paper and index finger of her other hand keeping place in her notebook.

Rathlin quite rightly kept quiet, as he knew better than to

disturb his wife when she was engrossed in something as important as this task. Both he and Angus flopped on the couch and the pony-tailed head of The Secret Society of Dragon Protectors studied his young protector carefully as Angus stared thoughtfully into the fireplace. Rathlin knew the lad was troubled by the thought of tackling Felspar and he knew he must bolster the young protector's confidence but now was not the time and he placed that conversation to one side for now.

"Finished!" stated Aurora Tek, suddenly bringing Rathlin back from his rumination.

"What have you got dear?" he asked.

"Angus, do you remember the two sites in Wellshire?" she asked rousing the lad out of his own ponderings. "Well we've not checked on those yet and there are others, so I've made two lists" she went on not waiting for his answer.

"Why two lists?" asked Angus quietly.

"Well this one…" she handed it to Rathlin, "has the most likely candidates… three of them to be exact, and this one has the other two that might be possible but don't quite fit… However I'm sure it must be one of those" she explained pointing to the list Rathlin was studying.

Rathlin suddenly jumped up and kissed his wife.

"Aurora you're a genius… and there's the Cornish one as

well… Don't worry Angus, I'm not giving up finding this time travel portal!" he stated confidently, "however it will have to wait until morning as it is way past our bedtime I think!"

Angus acknowledged this by yawning drowsily as he bade them goodnight. The young blond haired protector trudged up the stairs to the guest bedroom that Mrs T had prepared for him. Soon he was tucked up in a large four poster bed watching the moonlight shine through his window onto the white wall opposite.

The next morning Angus awoke having whiled away the night tossing and turning in bed as images of moonlight turned into the purple light he saw in his previous dreams. The dark blue dragon he had seen before, wavered intermittently throughout, but never long enough for Angus to gain any clue as to its identity.

Angus walked wearily downstairs feeling very sleepy despite the powerful shower's best efforts to invigorate him. Rathlin had already eaten breakfast and was coming back from walking the dogs when Angus traipsed into the kitchen.

"Good morning Angus!" he said brightly.

"Morning" was the unenthusiastic reply.

"What's the matter lad, didn't you sleep well?"

"Not really… some stupid dreams kept me awake" replied

Angus.

"Was it anything we should know about?" asked Rathlin suddenly more solemn.

The younger Tek brother had learned to take Angus' dreams most seriously as it was apparent he was tuned into the dragons more than most.

"No it was just random stuff... nothing important" replied Angus as he fetched some cereal from the cupboard.

Rathlin decided to let it go for now and discussed the trip they had to make today to visit the three sites Mrs T had chosen.

"So we will head for Cornwall first and then Wellshire which will set you and Pyrra up nicely for going home..." he said to Angus.

Someone lurked in the shadow of the corridor to the Great Hall listening to the conversation with great interest. The urge to indulge in a habitual ritual was curtailed lest someone heard which would give away their position.

Rathlin finished planning the trip with Angus and began to make some tea for Mrs T as she would arrive back from the mainland very soon. She had gone to get some groceries using her trusty old dragon and he was amused by the thought of her telling the old boy, Tejas, to fly using normal time. Angus finished off his breakfast and returned to the Great Hall through the corridor with his head down.

"Hello… its Angus isn't it?" said a voice startling him. Angus looked up and saw the man he had met in the previous week, he could not remember his name but overcoming his initial shock he managed a polite reply.

"Hi… yeah… how are you?"

"I'm very well… sorry I startled you, we've met before… I'm Robert, Robert Fitch… You probably don't remember…"

"Yes I do… I'm just a little tired that's all Mr Fitch" replied Angus.

"Please call me Robert" said the man. "Tell me have you seen Meredith yet? I'm supposed to meet her here this morning and it's not like her to be late!"

"I'm here Robert!" called a voice from the cellar doorway as Meredith appeared smiling. "I was just making sure my dragon was comfortable" she added as she walked confidently across the hall.

Angus listened politely as the pair talked about business and other such matters that did not interest him in any way. In fact it was sending him to sleep as they sat in front of the fire, the heat combining with the boring conversation about commerce and industry.

"So what other types of weapon do you sell Robert?" asked

Meredith sparking Angus' attention for a second.

"We don't sell weapons really… more security and stealth products like electronic listening devices… our latest gadgets allow you to see people for miles and hear the conversations they have" he replied.

"Cool!" said Angus unable to help himself.

"It was Robert whom I bought the sat-link from" said Meredith smiling.

"Oh that old thing was army surplus… they practically give it away once it's classed as outdated!" he replied laughing. "It's still state of the art technology though!"

Aurora Tek appeared through the corridor removing her gloves. She had just returned with the groceries at the back door and Rathlin was putting them away. When she saw the visitors Mrs T stopped dead.

"Good Morning Angus… Sorry I didn't know we had guests!" she said rather frostily.

Angus assumed by her tone, that Mrs T was not too happy at having unexpected visitors and decided to change the subject.

"Hi Mrs T, how was your journey?" he asked.

"Very pleasant Angus, thank you… Rathlin told me you didn't sleep very well, are you okay dear?" she asked concerned.

"Yeah I'm fine just some stupid dreams" he replied.

"Have you dreamt about the fugitive dragon again Angus?" asked Meredith, oozing interest.

"Em… no I didn't. Like I told Rathlin, it was just random stuff" replied Angus, then changing the subject again. "Is Rathlin ready to go?" he asked Mrs T.

"Have you found the portal yet?" asked Meredith interrupting again and drawing a dark look from Mrs T.

"Not yet but we're checking some possibilities today" he replied.

"Rathlin is waiting for you out the back" said Aurora testily. "Off you go and get Pyrra" she added as she ushered him down the corridor.

Angus grabbed his jacket and backpack as he ran out the back door to the small garden outside the kitchen. Rathlin stood on the other side of the hedge with the dragon saddle. He called for Cyru who groaned, sensing another long journey coming on.

"C'mon Cyru, time to go!"
Meanwhile in his favourite patch of Blue Dragon Fire Cyru muttered,

"Here we go again…" to Pyrra who had already stood up and was stretching her wings.

Both dragons lumbered over to Rathlin and Angus jumped up onto Pyrra's back. They both watched as Cyru sucked his chest in and Rathlin threw the Tek saddle over the reluctant dragon's back and pulled the straps to fasten it tight. Angus and Pyrra did not bother with the saddle much; the only time they used it was during the Trials.

"Where are we heading first, Rathlin?" asked Angus.

"I think we'll start with the Cornish one that you thought looked like a launch pad... Zennor Quoit..." said Rathlin who was keen to get on with the quest.

Cyru rolled his eyes at Pyrra as Rathlin tightened the saddle another notch.

The quartet was soon flying over the rolling hills and plains of Wellshire which spread out below them like a green counterpane. As they flew side by side down the mainland coast of Britain to the most south-westerly county of England. Angus scanned the ground below them, looking for the large flat covering stone but then he remembered Mrs T saying that a farmer had rearranged the prehistoric monument in the 19th century in order to use it as a wall for his cattle shed. At last they spotted a large pile of stones and circled it before they landed on the grass, surprising and scattering the cows that grazed nearby. The cows had felt a sudden whoosh but could not see anything, but as with most animals they could sense danger. The protectors dismounted the dragons and Rathlin asked Angus to read aloud the notes about the megalith as he strode around it running his hands over the stones.

"The Quoit is a fine example of the Cornish version of Portal Dolmen. The Cornish form involves the addition of two flanking stones either side of the front closure stone, these flanking stones create a small enclosed space or forecourt at the front of the tomb…" read Angus aloud.
He stared at the ancient stones and wondered if the word portal had any relevance to their search in this case.

"You know lad I think we'll know when we're in the right place… and I'm afraid this isn't it" he concluded. "Come on let's head up to Wellshire and find this Devil's Den."

The dragon's made good time back to Wellshire and landed deftly in a field with the stubble of wheat. Angus was intrigued by the name and he could not help wondering what would be waiting for them. Devil's Den actually consisted of two standing stones with a large one lying across the top like a lintel. Mrs T had told them that this was what the eminent Professor 'What's his name' imagined the inside of round barrows to be like. The whole thing acted as a sort of support structure for the ancient burial site, which was then covered in chalk and eventually through time, grass. Angus recalled the former librarian telling him they had sprung up all over the British Isles like warts, and many contained traces of human, and sometimes animal bones, as well as bits of pottery. This one however stood quite alone, uncovered and just as she had described, Angus could see two upright stones with a larger one balanced precariously on the top. At least it looked unstable, but then he reasoned that it had stood in precisely the same position for thousands of years. This was surely the prehistoric burial chamber they were seeking, rising up like a giant mushroom in the middle of a field.

"I believe this dates from about the same time as Man Barrow at West Flippance and is probably between two and three thousand years old" commented Rathlin.

Angus suppressed a smile knowing that he was not the only one receiving history lessons from the former librarian.

"But this can't be right either" said Rathlin, "its not big enough to fit a dragon through... What Finian told me is making more sense now... we're looking for some sort of ancient stone doorway."

Angus was not sure about the doorway part but he was sure in his heart that he would recognise the portal when he saw it!

Taking to the air once again they were soon in the familiar

air space above Marnham. Cyru scoured the landscape below and soon picked up a valley, perhaps once an ancient riverbed, strewn with boulders. The dragons followed the dots of grey stones, which broke through the grass in random patterns. Indeed from a great height it was hard to distinguish the sheep from the stones and Angus sincerely hoped that Pyrra or Cyru were not feeling hungry. They swooped in low over another field and at the same time they saw two huge upright pillars standing in the field. Angus was reminded of ancient goalposts, quite a distance apart.

They alighted close by and Angus immediately noticed both Pyrra's and Cyru's heart stones glowing fiercely on their chests. More disturbingly the Dragonore changed colour dramatically from its usual aquamarine to a dark and resonant purple.

"Hey what's up with my Dragonore?" called Cyru. "I think it's faulty!" he watched the colour change as he approached the ancient monument.

Angus had never seen Dragonore change colour before, except of course for the Cor Stan when it was all charged up, or when it was near other dragons. He felt the pouch around his neck burning his skin and his Dragonore was heating up really fiercely too. However, this was nothing like those occasions. It was like some form of superheat and the colour change was very different from anything he had ever seen before. Except he *had* seen it before! This was the purple light invading his dreams of late and it indicated they had found objective of their journey. Angus looked at the rock pillars again now that he was closer and he knew immediately.

"Rathlin, this is the portal…" he shouted, "It's the two rocks in my dream… this is the gateway, I'm sure of it!"

"Stone the crows!" exclaimed Rathlin, using one of his favourite expressions when no other words could convey his emotion. "It's certainly wide enough for a dragon to fly through! I think you're right… we've found the portal!"

Chapter 14

'Uncertainty'

Angus explored the lichen-covered pillars, poking and prodding all the nooks and crannies as if he were expecting a secret door to open within the ancient Saracen stones. He wondered what secrets lay undiscovered, waiting to be found after thousands of years. He recalled Mrs T telling him that Saracen meant troublesome and he wondered if these stones would prove to be exactly what their name suggested.

"This must be a special place indeed to make the mineral react so violently" exclaimed Pyrra as she inspected her Dragonore.

Cyru was already bored and wandered closer to the stones already planning a trip back to Dundee in his mind. He scratched his back on the outside of one of the great uprights.

"Mind you don't knock it over Cyru!" called Rathlin frowning.

"Look what's happening to your Dragonore!" shouted Angus his attention drawn to the blue dragon by Rathlin's comment.

They all stared at Cyru's Heart Stone which indeed looked as if it might combust, it was glowing so fiercely. Purple flashes of light emanated from the Dragonore and once again Angus was reminded of his dream but he still did not know how time travel could ever be possible.

"Mind you don't pass through time" warned Rathlin laughing at Cyru, "I don't want to lose you in history."

"The Dragonore is the key to this door" Pyrra said slowly, as if remembering something from a time when her magical powers were fully operational.

"How does that work then?" asked Angus with interest.

"I can't remember but I think Godroi will know… he has the knowledge passed on from Ward Barfoot" she replied.

"Hopefully we can find Felspar before he finds this portal, but if the Ward doesn't remember, then I can't understand how Felspar would know how it works" said Rathlin.

"We cannot underestimate him… he may have gained the knowledge by some other means!" replied Pyrra sagely.

"What next then?" Angus asked.

"I will report back to Finian and Godroi and find out what they want us to do, but in the meantime we must continue to search for Felspar" he replied seriously.

Angus was not sure they would be able to find the black dragon, as he had totally evaded them thus far. For one, he had acquired Dragonore from Krubera, and large amounts of it! He was also being helped by someone that the SSDP did not know of. Clearly it was not Fergus, but that person obviously knew Krubera, and where to find the Cor Stan within the cavern system.

"Rathlin, how many protectors have been to Krubera?" he asked suddenly.

"I don't know Angus... maybe all of them... Why?"

"I guess we're looking for someone who knows their way around the caves, so it must be a protector!" replied Angus looking thoughtful.

"You could be on to something there lad" agreed Rathlin, "but it could be that Felspar had given them instructions."

"I thought of that, but someone new would be afraid going in there for the first time. At least, I think they would" replied Angus logically.

"I didn't consider it like that..." said Rathlin, "I will get to work on who has been there and we can start to check through them."

"We had better get you home Angus, it's getting late!" interjected Pyrra breaking into the discussion.

She had listened to her young protectors theories on Felspar's accomplice and was sure he was correct. Clearly the SSDP had another bad element within its ranks and she would have to speak with Rathlin about future recruitment policies. Going their separate ways, Rathlin and Cyru to Calmor and Angus and Pyrra back to Kynton to drop Angus off, the four reassured themselves that Godroi was in no immediate danger. Whatever Felspar was planning, he did not know the location of the portal and that was a comforting thought.

Some time later, Rathlin marched into the Great Hall excited by the news he brought with him. It was mid afternoon and he was surprised to still find Meredith and Robert at Calmor. A few other young protectors entered with Liam as they followed Rathlin to find out why the head of the SSDP was so energised.

"Well, it seems everyone is here today..." said Rathlin looking around, "has anyone seen my wife?"

"She's in the kitchen Rathlin" purred Meredith. "You look excited... what is it?"

"I have some good news... Ah Aurora my dear, we've found it!" he said to Mrs T as she walked into the Great Hall to see what all the noise was about.

"Oh fantastic!" she exclaimed. "So was it one of the sites in Wellshire?" she asked.

Rathlin remembered Angus' theory had that the SSDP had a spy who worked for Felspar. He looked around the hall quickly taking in the faces of those present and now felt reluctant to answer, however he could not avoid the question.

"Yes it was" he answered quietly.

"I knew it would be there!" she squealed, "It's such a wonderful place for that sort of thing… which site was it?" Studying the expectant faces before him, Rathlin could see the mixture of anticipation, eagerness and interest on the faces of the protectors.

"I'm tired and thirsty dear let's go to the kitchen for a nice cuppa and I'll tell you all about it" he replied evasively. "Lads, can you make sure the dragons are looked after and I will catch up with you later?"

The old kettle whistled on the cast iron range that dominated the Tek's kitchen, as the water boiled for tea. Rathlin sat at the table, deep in thought.

"Penny for your thoughts?" asked Aurora.

"Eh… oh sorry dear… I was just pondering something Angus said" he replied despondently.

"What was that?" she asked as she sat down at the table beside him looking concerned.

"He thinks we may have a spy in the SSDP… Someone helping Felspar" he replied seriously.

"Surely not dear… He really does have an overactive imagination" she smiled.

"Unfortunately I believe he is right" replied Rathlin. "It's the only way Felspar could have obtained the Dragonore… It just didn't occur to me before."

"But it could still be Fergus… he might be lying" she said.

"No Aurora… I saw the look on that lad's face and I would put money on the fact he was not lying" replied Rathlin vehemently.

The kettle rattled violently on the stove drawing their attention to the loud whistling they had managed to ignore during their conversation and Mrs T rushed to remove it.

In the Great Hall, two of the adult protectors prepared to leave Calmor for home, and as one of them put on a large black coat they spied a piece of paper on the mantelpiece above the great fireplace. The individual casually looked at it with their back to the large room and read the finely crafted script on the page. It was written by the hand of someone who took pleasure in the written word and it listed three prehistoric sites in England. The locations were carefully explained in detail with instructions on how to get there and it was slipped casually into the pocket of the coat with a sleight of hand.

"Are you ready to go then?" asked Robert Fitch.

"Certainly!" replied Meredith Quinton-Jones, smiling.

They walked through the hidden door on the mural wall that led to the dragon sanctuary below.

Chapter 15

'Purple Flash'

"So that's about all I have to report" said Rathlin after he had finished his lengthy explanation of the day's events. Godroi and Finian stood silently side by side in Krubera, as the image of Rathlin wavered slightly on the screen. Finian was first to speak.

"What do you think?" he asked Godroi.

"Felspar has not left yet, but I think Angus is somehow correct and we would be wise to observe the lad's instincts on this…" replied the Ward sagely, "Rathlin, you must make that list and perhaps we will be lucky enough to spot the culprit, however I doubt it will be so easy to find the guilty person as they will have covered their tracks!"

"What about Felspar?" Rathlin asked.

"He is not a threat just yet, and I sense he has still not found the portal… however we must maintain the search for him as he is far too dangerous to be left at large" said Godroi. "I will consider the workings of the portal and attempt to recall it's usage from my inherited memories."

Rathlin bade his brother and the Ward goodbye and switched the sat-link off. He felt angry and betrayed that the SSDP had found and recruited someone who would abuse their position of trust within the organisation. He struggled to comprehend how destroying the SSDP would provide gain for such a person but he was determined to stop them. Rathlin strode to the castle to find a phone and brief the only protector he could truly trust, other than his brother and his wife.

Angus sank into his bed and curled his long limbs under his duvet, exhausted but relieved that Godroi's past and therefore the dragon's future, was safe for now. Rathlin's call had confirmed that Godroi believed the black dragon had not yet found the portal and that comforted him a little. Rathlin needed them to continue the search for Felspar, but for now Angus just wanted to sleep.

The morning sunshine blazed through the curtains as the noise of his alarm clock buzzed in his ears. Angus had slept better than the previous night in Calmor but he had still dreamt of something he could not quite grasp. He considered the fragmented images, trying to make sense of them as he got ready for school, when the dark blue dragon's face entered his head for a second. He wondered if he did dream about that dragon and he strove to recall more. The stone pillars were there, but he assumed that was due to his visit to them earlier that day. What did strike him as odd was, the image of a piece of paper being handed to a dragon. The hand was gloved in black and the claw was black. In fact, Angus had almost believed he was dreaming in black and white until he remembered something about the handwriting on the paper. It only occurred to him now what he had been looking at in his dream, the writing was in blue!

School passed in a blur of robotic participation until Angus could meet with Pyrra later that day. The message from Rathlin discussed, the dragon sensed her young minder had something more to tell her.

"You've had another dream I see" she said wisely.

"How did you know?" asked Angus surprised.

Pyrra just smiled and tapped a long clawed digit to the side of her head. Angus explained the fragments he could recall and theorised on what they meant to him.

"So you believe Felspar knows about the portal?" asked Pyrra thoughtfully.

"I don't know… it's a bit confusing, but I guess I think he does…" Angus replied miserably, "I just don't know what to do about it Pyrra!"

"Well I do… We can work this out as long as we stick together, and we find Felspar before he has a chance to get to Godroi!" replied Pyrra as she placed her fore claw gently on his shoulder. "Tomorrow we will go and find Caedmon again to see if he has any more news, okay?"

Angus nodded in agreement, pleased to have Pyrra's support, and knowing at least they were doing something positive.

That night Angus' dreams were again fragmented by the same images, this time, appearing more real than before. He explained them once again to Pyrra as they flew to meet Argent and Georgina but this time Pyrra kept her own counsel. The four took off from Marnham and Angus viewed the church from his vantage point on Pyrra's back. He could see the differences in the town from the past, as the picture of the ancient village was etched in his mind from his visions. Soon they located Caedmon on his gatepost, just as Angus finished bringing Georgina up to speed on events.

"Caedmon, are you there?" called Pyrra.

Like the last time they visited the main gate of the mansion, the dragon was quiet and had seemingly either not heard or was ignoring them.

"Caedmon, stop messing about, come down here now!" shouted Argent rather rudely.

Immediately the dragon morphed from the statuette and landed clumsily onto the ground next to Georgina who staggered out of the way to stand behind Angus.

"And just what do you want here? I told you back then and I'll tell you now… I want nothing to do with you… you USURPER!" said Caedmon spitting the last word venomously.

"Angus, what's he going on about?" asked Georgina worriedly.

"I think our grey friend has just called Argent a thief!" smiled Angus.

"Thief!" laughed Argent, "I'm no thief, just smarter and quicker than you!"

Caedmon looked furious and Angus thought this was about to turn into a fight until Pyrra stepped in.

"Now, now boys, let's not be too hasty!" she said stepping between them. "What's all this about?"

"That fool of a dragon stole my hiding place!" snapped Caedmon angrily.

"It wasn't like that at all…" replied Argent, "I merely found an empty hiding place and took it… how was I supposed to know that Caedmon had his eye on it!"

"It was mine and you know it… Godroi said I could use it if I wanted to and then you moved in without asking… I asked you to leave and you refused!" shouted the grey dragon rearing up. Argent roared and reared in response which caused Georgina to grab Angus in terror, but Pyrra was having none of it.

"Enough of this stupidity!" she bellowed. "I cannot believe what I am hearing... you've been here for over seven hundred years, haven't you been happy here?" she said turning to Caedmon.

The grey dragon relaxed his posture returning his fore claws to the ground.

"Of course I have, but that's not the point" he replied. "He took it without asking and he thinks he is so superior!"

"Look, I'm sorry I took it, but I needed a hiding place and that one was vacant. I would have been nice to you back then, but you were extremely nasty when you came looking for the gargoyle and I just didn't like it... at least you had a home!" replied Argent, lowering his own defences slightly and explaining his side of the story.

Pyrra managed to calm both of them down and after some time managed to ask about Felspar.

"I told you before I have not seen Felspar and even if I did, I wouldn't tell you about it!" replied the ignorant grey dragon before he morphed back into his hiding place.

The foursome walked back to the roadside, all extremely confused by what they had just witnessed. Angus and Pyrra were surprised to find Caedmon so unhelpful and not in the same frame of mind as on their previous meeting. In fact he was the complete opposite again and the whole episode left them feeling rather puzzled by his behaviour.

"Why would he suddenly turn nasty again after helping us before?" asked Angus.

"I don't know but it's very strange… Perhaps we're reading too much into this and he is just not happy with people visiting his hiding place!" said Pyrra as she tried to cheer the lad up but his mood did not change until Georgina spoke.

"Wow Argent I didn't know you were such a bad dragon" she teased.

"I… I'm not! Caedmon is just crazy!" he protested.
Angus smiled at Argent's attempt to explain his innocence and he imagined the silver dragon being confronted at the church, but that thought only reminded him of the duel between Godroi and Felspar.

Angus went home that night rather disappointed by their lack of headway on the whereabouts of the wayward dragon and wondered if he had missed something. The next two days dragged with no sign of Felspar anywhere and Angus knew something was wrong. Putting his key in the door, he called a greeting to his parents as he entered the hallway, but it reverberated around the empty house. Angus remembered it was Thursday and delivery night. His mum had left him a note on the telephone table written in her neat handwriting. Angus picked it up and read, 'Fergus called' and then a number. The young protector's hands trembled as he punched out the number, almost misdialling. Fergus answered at once.

"Hi Fergus it's me, Angus" he said.

"Angus, Felspar's been back to see me and he warned him to keep away from you, Rathlin and anyone else from the SSDP!" he blurted sounding worried.

"When was this?" asked Angus urgently.

"Just today, but he did say something else… He said it wouldn't matter soon, as everything would be different in a day or two… What does that mean?" asked the former protector.

"No idea, but I will let Rathlin know… Thanks Fergus… and watch yourself!" he replied carefully.

"I tried Rathlin's number several times but the line is not working… good luck Angus" said Fergus.

Angus was surprised as the older lad sounded sincere.

"Thanks… listen don't worry about Felspar we're going to get him!" replied Angus trying to sound confident.

"I'm not worried now… we're moving house soon and he won't be able to find me… See ya!"

Angus privately wondered how they could stop the malevolent dragon. He quickly dialled Calmor Castle only to confirm what

Fergus had already told him. The line was dead, so he could only keep trying until he got through to the head of the SSDP and give him the bad news. If his dream was correct, and what Fergus had told him was true. Felspar already knew the location of the portal and was about to use it. He tried the number several times again before sliding down the wall beside the small table. He dejectedly re-tried the number after lifting the phone down to the floor beside him and began to feel helpless as time ticked on.

Unaware that he had closed his eyes, Angus was soon flying through the clouds and down towards the rain-soaked hillsides. The grass swept up before him and he levelled out as he flew past the church at Marnham. Serpent Tor appeared and disappeared as quickly as it arrived only to be replaced by another familiar sight. Angus recognised the stones in the valley first and then the standing stones appeared in the distance. The dragon looked at its chest as the Dragonore began to glow, not blue, but purple. Angus tried to scream out when he realised that the dragon was not Pyrra but the black dragon himself. The boy inadvertently flinched in his sleep, fearing a re-run of the fight scene with himself sitting in what would be the best seat in the house. However, Felspar was not in battle mode and the villain flew at great speed towards the pillars. The purple light brightened and blinded all around Felspar until it was impossible to see anything but a purple flash. The dragon had disappeared!

Chapter 16

'A Grave Endeavour'

Angus awoke with a start, unsure of where he was. He wondered whether he had actually witnessed the whole episode or if he had dreamt it; the entire thing seemed so real. He had kicked the phone over and could hear the receiver bleeping loudly on the floor, demanding to be replaced. Coming to his senses Angus grabbed the handset and righted it. The house was in darkness and it was obvious his Mum and Dad had not come home yet. He turned on the hall light and began to dial Calmor once more.

"Hello Tek residence" said Mrs T.

"At last… I've been trying your number for ages!" said Angus. "I have news about Felspar, is Rathlin there?"

"Oh… yes he is… we've just had a bad storm and the island's electricity failed… he had to fix the sat-link… hold on and I'll get him!" she replied.

Angus heard her place the phone on the table and then her footsteps clipping across the stone floor of the Great Hall. He tried to gets his thoughts in order to make sure he did not miss anything out. Apart from the call from Fergus, Angus needed to recall the dream correctly.

"Angus what's the matter lad… what's the news?" asked Rathlin picking up the receiver.

Angus explained about Fergus, then the dream and urged Rathlin to contact Godroi at once.

Five minutes later Angus anxiously paced inside the hallway of his home as he waited for the return call from Rathlin. He already knew what the outcome was going to be but he needed to hear exactly what action would be required. The phone rang, jolting him from internal remonstrations.

"Hello Angus… sorry for the delay but the signal is still not too good. I have quickly explained to Godroi what you told me and he wants to speak to you… I will put the mobile on loudspeaker."

"Hello Angus, can you hear me?" said Godroi slowly.

"Yes I can Godroi" replied Angus clearly.

"Good… It is grave news indeed that Felspar has gone through the portal and as you have seen it, I have no doubt that it has happened!" said the Ward. "We must now consider drastic action of our own to protect the present as we know it!" he added. "We need to send someone through the portal to stop Felspar and that task falls to you and Pyrra!"

The silence that followed seemed to go on forever, but Angus was only conscious of his own breathing as his thoughts and feelings reeled.

"I'm sorry Godroi, but as head of the SSDP, I cannot let Angus go into such a dangerous situation… I will go in his place!" interjected Rathlin.

Angus' heart leapt at the thought of not having to go, but he instantly felt ashamed of doing so, and while he tried to find the courage to speak up, Godroi beat him to it.

"No Rathlin, I am sorry, but it has to be Angus" answered the Ward firmly.

"But, he's still a boy…" pushed Rathlin, "no offence lad, but that dragon is vicious!"

"I wish I could explain it to you both, but you must trust me when I tell you, Angus must follow Felspar with Pyrra… there is no other way!"

The Ward had spoken with such authority that both Rathlin and Angus were stunned into silence.

"Well lad it's up to you… are you up for this?" asked Rathlin over the loudspeaker.

"I… think so… but we don't know how to use the portal" replied Angus quietly.

"I will explain it all, but remember Angus, your bravery and quick wits are your greatest weapon!"

Angus was not sure what that meant, but he was used to the

dragon Wards saying things that confused him.

"We dragons need a lot of Dragonore to be able to use the portal and since you may not have enough at Calmor the rest will have to come from Krubera…" continued the Ward, "Rathlin will no doubt help us there."

"Of course, I will be there tomorrow" confirmed Rathlin.

"Although Pyrra can help transport you to the correct time we believe Felspar will attack me, she cannot take the life of another dragon and my past self will not do this either" Angus heard the Ward continue. "You must devise a means of stopping Felspar using your initiative and remember you have the advantage now… my only warning to you is this… we dragons have not permitted the use of the portal because of the danger it poses, I must reiterate that this is an exception to the rule!"

"Why don't you use time travel more often?" asked Angus.

"It is extremely dangerous and it is not ordinarily permitted to mess about with history" replied the Ward.

"But why not send all the dragons to the future, to a time when it's safe?" he quizzed intelligently.

"A good point Angus, and one that Finian and I have discussed already. It is true we await the time when dragons may be able to inhabit the earth freely, but the future is never certain and therefore travel to the future was forbidden. It should also be considered that if dragons do not exist in the present then how will it ever become safe for them in the future… We may have hidden ourselves in the past, Angus but we are still very much a part of it!" The wise dragon paused for breath and then went on. "We would not normally change history to suit our own purposes as it is our way to allow things to happen. In this case, however, Felspar is breaking all the rules and so you must stop him at any cost!"

"I don't know how I'm going to do that!" laughed Angus nervously.

"You will find a way" replied the Ward his voice confident, "Remember that faith is an assurance of things hoped for… and we have great faith in you. Your destiny is interlinked with ours!"

The conversation ended with Rathlin and Finian making plans to obtain the necessary amount of Dragonore for the task. Angus was too engrossed in his own thoughts to take much heed of what was being said and had to hang up when he heard his parents' Kleanware van pull into the driveway.

Angus did not sleep that night and the next day at school passed in a daze due to his lack of sleep. He could not focus on any lesson and was chastised by several of his teachers for not paying attention in their lessons. He trudged home feeling altogether miserable and not even fit for the journey to Piggleston. He still had to break the bad news to Pyrra and he did not relish that conversation at all. After greeting the green dragon in the usual manner with cough candy the dejected lad slumped down against one of the trees in the place where they always met. Pyrra touched down lightly in the space near him and immediately realised all was not well with her protector.

"What's the matter Angus?" she asked with concern in her voice.

Angus took his time to answer as he was a cauldron of feelings all mixed up with fear, rage, disbelief and distress.

"It's Felspar…" he groaned, "He's gone through the portal!"

"When?" she asked looking confused, "How do you know this?"

Her young protector explained the phone calls with Fergus and Godroi; the dream and Godroi's insistence that they must follow the treacherous dragon back through time to somehow save the day.

"I'm sure we will not be alone Angus, Godroi will have a plan!" she said trying to console the young lad.

"That's the problem, he doesn't… and he thinks I will come up with something!" replied Angus woefully.

Pyrra understood how Angus must be feeling as she now shared his trepidation at the thought of tracking down the foul beast. She instead focused on the present and began to make practical plans with Angus for their trip to Calmor the next day.

Hurrying to the dragon sanctuary as quickly as dragon time enabled, Pyrra and Angus spoke very little. Both were locked deep in their own thoughts regarding the dangerous journey they now knew they had to make. As soon as they landed Angus told Pyrra she must go at once to the lighthouse where she would receive instructions from Godroi via the satellite link. The Ward wanted to enlighten Pyrra as to how to enter the Wellshire portal and arrive at the exact moment in history they required.

"You can only travel back to a specified time and place that you have already chosen…" described Godroi to Pyrra who had her head stuck through the doorway of the lighthouse cottage.

Normally Angus would have found the sight comical, but somehow he did not feel very light hearted at the moment.

"Are you sure of the dates Godroi?" asked Pyrra interrupting the Ward's flow.

"Of course I am… I am not that old just yet Pyrra!" replied Godroi smiling. "Now where was I? Ah yes, now complete concentration is required on the date chosen. In fact it is essential! One stray thought and you may end up in an entirely different era from which it may not be possible to return!" The last words of the golden dragon rung repeatedly in Angus' head and haunted his thoughts for the remainder of the day.

Chapter 17

'Strength of Will'

Furnished with the vital information they required, Angus and Pyrra were soon on their way southwest to the pillar stones in Wellshire, to rendezvous with Rathlin and Cyru. Soon the portal was in sight and the pit of Angus' stomach knotted with nerves.

"Angus, Pyrra... I was beginning to wonder if you were going to turn up!" greeted Rathlin, laughing as they landed.

"Godroi's instructions took a little longer to explain than we thought" replied Pyrra looking pensively towards the two standing stones nearby.

"You're happy with the year he chose?" asked Rathlin looking concerned, "Only he wasn't sure the first time I asked him..."

"What do you mean not sure? He only gave me one date!" replied Pyrra now disturbed.

"It's nothing... I just wanted to make sure..."

"No tell me... What did he say?" she pushed.

"Well he was torn between two dates, 1237 and 1238 but if he is wrong you will be one year too late!"

Pyrra considered this for a moment before answering.

"Then I will have to trust his judgement and hope that he is correct!" she replied.

"You're right... Sorry I should not have mentioned it..." added Rathlin sheepishly, "I should have more faith."

Several members of The Secret Society of Dragon Protectors had turned out for the momentous event. The moment Pyrra entered the portal would make her only the fourth dragon in history to use time travel. The first two journeys were by an ancient Ward whose name was now held in the depths of Godroi's knowledge and the third was Felspar. Until the black dragon had done the unthinkable, the portal had not been used for over two thousand years. Even then the ancient dragon Ward had only used it as an experiment and Godroi would not elaborate on the dragon's adventure through time but would only confirm that the results of his time travel initiated the rules just recently remembered.

One by one the other protectors and dragons present walked up to the intrepid pair passing on wishes of good luck. Angus could almost taste the tension in the air and when Georgina appeared from a tent the lump that had grown in his throat threatened to choke him.

"Hi Angus... how do you feel?" she asked quietly as if treading on eggshells.

The young protector wanted to confess his fear to the girl that had quickly become one of his closest confidants but he knew that was not what she wanted to hear.

"I'm okay" he lied, trying to mask his self doubt.

"Are you ready to go Angus?" asked Pyrra saving him from further awkward questioning.

Angus took a deep breath and nodded his head, smiling bravely.

As they took off for the point Godroi told them they must start from, Angus could see the field spread before them with the tents of the SSDP pitched near the pillars and the rock strewn area between. Seated on Pyrra's back at the top end of the valley of stones, Angus looked down across the ploughed fields to the ancient gateway below and felt it begin to rain. Pyrra was quite apprehensive, not being sure what to expect once they reached the two standing stones, or the other side. Her earlier conversation with Rathlin had rattled her confidence in what she was doing and she was tempted to go for the earlier date. The only consolation she could think of was if they were wrong she could use the portal again and arrive at the correct moment in time they required. Focusing on that thought, the green dragon tried to keep calm for Angus' sake as she could sense his own doubts, but she could also feel his strength of will and taking heart from her young protector's inner power, Pyrra concentrated her mind on midsummer solstice June 12th 1238.

That was the chosen time to intercept Godroi and hopefully Felspar at Marnham. Angus was nervous and excited in anticipation of what was to come. He wondered whether passing through the portal would physically hurt, or if his ears would pop like in an aeroplane. He would not have to wait long to find out as Rathlin walked towards them having just landed with Cyru. Angus zipped up his jacket and pulled the hood round his ears. From a distance his actions were like that of a knight preparing for his launch into battle. As Rathlin paced around giving out last minute instructions to Pyrra he handed over the extra Dragonore and Pyrra held it tightly in her fore claws. Angus adjusted his backpack making sure it was secure and tightened his sweaty grip on Pyrra's back.

It was now time and on Rathlin's command Pyrra sprang upwards, launched off the crest of the gully and plunged down into the rain soaked valley at high speed. The protectors gathered near the megaliths and they saw the big piece of mineral change colour from bright blue to vivid purple and then everything seemed to happen at once. They onlookers saw Pyrra and Angus turn into what looked like an enormous firework as they sped towards the pillars. Then dragon and boy moved into dragon time and a purple flash rocketed toward the gateway, passing between the posts at high speed. Then they saw no more.

Angus watched Pyrra leap into the gully and as he pinned his body to her back, the purple light blinded him, just as it did in his visions. The glow intensified as she sped towards the standing stones and the world blurred as she moved into dragon time. The Dragonore hanging around his neck burned, increasing in strength as the portal loomed ahead. The light brightened so much that Angus was forced to close his eyes, burying his face into the security of Pyrra's rough scaly neck. He was so preoccupied that he was completely unaware of a slight popping noise as they left the present and plummeted headlong into...

Chapter 18

'Stanbury Fete'

The protectors stood around looking at each other not quite sure of what they had just witnessed.

"I don't believe it! They actually did it!" shouted Rathlin as he punched the air.

Not knowing what else to do, he organised Liam, Georgina and Kadin into pitching the remaining tents in the bleak ploughed field. You could be forgiven for thinking Rathlin was once a Scoutmaster as he certainly acted like one. He soon had a fire going and Liam knocked up a tripod so they could boil water for a reviving cup of tea; an SSDP ritual that always involved flapjacks. They had no idea how long the trip to the past was expected to take and nobody wanted to go anywhere in case they missed anything from the historic occasion.

The village of Stanbury stood in the middle of a small valley surrounded by fertile farmland. The peasants who lived in the simple homes made of wood were hard working folk who believed the seasons would fulfil their needs, providing they were celebrated in the correct manner. It was Midsummer Solstice and the Stanbury fete was in full swing. People wore the best clothes they had and some tied ribbons to them.

Minstrels played their music and the villagers danced, drank and ate in celebration of the summer season. It had been a mild winter and spring, indicating that the summers harvest would be a bumper one. The farmers were in good sprits and nothing could dampen the mood of the village.

Suddenly a blinding purple light shone from the direction of the ancient standing stones that the village owed its name to. The music paused as, one by one, the inhabitants turned to look at the strange light emanating from between the pillars; its intensity increasing so much that it forced them to cover their eyes.

Angus took a moment to focus as the light diminished and his eyes adjusted to the summer sunshine. They seemed to have literally crashed into the middle of some sort of fete and Angus stared in disbelief at the villagers standing motionless around them shielding their faces.

"Wow I didn't feel a thing Pyrra, but it looks like we've done it!" he shouted.

What the villagers saw was a large green dragon, with a strange looking rider, swoop through the middle of the two stone pillars, appearing from the blinding purple light. Shouts of 'Dragon!' and 'Demon!' filled the air and suddenly the village was filled with panic. People screamed and revellers scattered in every direction. Pandemonium broke out as women and children fled the scene, scattering food and spilling drink everywhere in their fear. Angus could see that these were mainly farm workers as he glanced around the village. Small houses, barns and sheds formed a rough square with a large space in the centre. Animal pens clustered around the open space where the fete was being held and the village was surrounded by crop filled fields and pastures. Chickens, sheep and other livestock ran wild amongst the revellers, adding to the panic and confusion as most of the people fled towards the trees, or hid behind buildings.

Pyrra turned to look at Angus with an amused look on her face.

"Well now, I've not had a reaction like that in a long while…" she held up the charred piece of Dragonore and looked at her chest, "I guess this is all spent and I am no longer invisible" she chuckled.

Angus frantically pulled his Dragonore pouch from under his coat and opened the bag. It was blackened and burnt from the use of the portal and his heart sank at the sight of his most prized possession destroyed.

"Don't worry about it Angus we will get you some more" said Pyrra seeing her protector's sadness.

Angus placed the now useless stone back in the pouch and tucked it away.

"Why were they shouting demon?" asked Angus as he watched some of the villagers peeking from behind their homes.

"Because you look so strange to them in your modern clothes and they have no other explanation..." she smiled, "and they probably reckon no human would be brave enough to ride a dragon!"

Angus noticed the some of the men of the village, as terrified-looking as the others, feigned bravery by grouping together to gesture towards the unwelcome invaders. They picked up the nearest implements as weapons, which being mainly farm workers proved to be all pointed and very sharp. Pyrra felt a sense of foreboding she had not experienced in many years; the feeling she was about to be attacked crept over her and instinct kicked in. One of the villagers had rounded up some men and was shouting instructions in Old English.

"I think we need to get out of here Angus! Those pitchforks are rather painful and I have no desire to experience them again!" called the affronted dragon to her friend.

She flapped her wings at the thronging villagers who, seeing their enemy falter, attacked with whatever they had to hand. It was the beginning of the Great Hibernation and many people believed in dragons at that time.

"I can't be absolutely sure but I think he's saying this is the second time the dragon has come to the village and they must drive it away now!" translated Pyrra.

The village leader thought about how unlucky they were to have a dragon appear in the middle of the festivities, but to have seen two dragons in the space of a couple of hours was just getting ridiculous. The first dragon arrived in the middle of the night and flew off before the alarm was raised by one of the locals on watch duty. No one else had seen the beast, so they accused the man of being drunk or dreaming.

At least this confirmed that the pair had landed in the roughly the right time, but it became apparent they could not stay in the village. They decided to retreat and wait for Felspar to appear elsewhere. Pyrra prepared to take off and fly out of reach of the emboldened farmers however she was not sure what to do next.

"Where do we go now?" asked Pyrra.

"We need more Dragonore… what about Krubera?" suggested Angus.

"Yes we do, and I think I know where we might get a small amount a little nearer to hand… My lair!" she replied enthusiastically.

"Cool Pyrra… I think we should get going *now*!' shouted Angus indicating the pitchforks that drew slowly nearer. The green dragon roared as she started to flap her wings at great speed just prior to take off and this stopped the attackers in their tracks. Angus bent into a low position on her back.

"LET"S GO!" he shouted to her.
She did not need any further encouragement and no sooner than she knew he was secure on her back, she was airborne.

Angus breathed a sigh of relief as they ascended into the safe cloud cover of the sky. As they flew, the pair began to see the funny side of what had just transpired, and relaxed into the flight. The amazing journey through the portal had used up all the magical properties of the Dragonore and Pyrra still carried the rock, now a dark cobalt colour. They needed to formulate a plan of action but firstly they needed the ability to remain

179

hidden or their journey in time would be very difficult indeed.

The Secret Society of Dragon Protectors

Chapter 19

'Timely Incursion'

Angus felt sure that Felspar had not appeared much before them. The reaction of the villagers appeared to be well organised since they were prepared to defend themselves so readily. Felspar would be visible to them like Pyrra was now and the black dragon would have to stay in hiding, or find himself hunted by the local people. A reassuring line of thought he shared with his scaly companion as they sped towards her mountain cave.

They left the spent, and now dull, mineral beside the entrance to Pyrra's lair. Boy and dragon edged cautiously inside, feeling their way in the darkness. Angus hoped Pyrra had enough Dragonore to make the return journey as the essential mineral they carried was all used up and they would be keen to be off as soon they had dealt with Felspar. Neither wished to hang around in the 13th century any longer than was necessary, especially as dragon baiting seemed to be the most popular pastime amongst the local peasants. Pyrra fired a jet of flame on the central rock of the cave and the warmth and glowing light revived their tired limbs. Settled in the seclusion of the familiar cave Pyrra further renewed her strength and powers by keeping very quiet and still. As she sat back on her haunches in what looked like a trance like state, Angus had the feeling they needed to be somewhere else.

"Pyrra I think we should check on Godroi now!" he said quietly but urgently.

She was not quite recovered but Pyrra understood the urgency of the situation. It was all a question of knowing when to be in the right place at the right time in order to intercept Felspar, but since they did not know where he was, or when he would strike, it seemed to Pyrra that they had an impossible task.

"Why now?" she asked opening her eyes.

"I… don't know… it's just a feeling…" replied Angus sheepishly.

"Well if we are going out flying, I need two things Angus…" said Pyrra standing up and stretching her wings outwards, "some food and Dragonore!"

She walked towards a small section of the cave that was strewn with small rocks and stared at them purposefully. Angus watched her pick one of the rocks up and claw the ground with her other claw. She picked something up and placed it on her chest as she turned towards Angus.

"Well that's one thing done!" said Pyrra as she threw something at Angus.

He caught it instinctively and looked at it.

"It's Dragonore!" he shouted. "Thanks Pyrra… that's cool!" The young protector took out his pouch from around his neck and placed his new Dragonore into it.

"Now I can go and eat without being seen" said Pyrra. Both boy and dragon were ravenous and Pyrra slipped outside to satiate her appetite on a wandering sheep from the nearby common land. Angus rummaged in his backpack and found a 21st century energy bar. He devoured it eagerly, barely taking off the wrapper.

Pyrra returned from her foray suitably fed and pleased that nobody saw her this time. They were keen to resume their task to ensure Godroi was safe and they were soon flying back down towards the village of Stanbury. Angus picked out a cart track which seemed to be heading in the right direction for Marnham and both were relieved to see that the peasants, busy cutting corn in the fields, took no notice of them.

As they approached from the air, Angus could see the spire and tower of the church of Marnham surrounded in parts by wooden frames that formed a sort of scaffold. The gargoyle for the roof was not yet in place and the stained glass windows, although in the solid stone wall of the church, were not all completed. They swooped in closer and saw that Godroi was not in the window as Pyrra landed softly close by. The jewel colours of the freshly made panes gleamed and Angus marvelled at how bright they were compared to how they looked in the future. Before Angus had a chance to dismount he experienced a terrible sense of déjà-vu and he spun around on Pyrra's back.

"Pyrra it's happening now!" called Angus upset.

The green dragon was shocked and knew from listening to Angus recounting his dreams what they were about to witness.

From the side of the church, Angus could hear the roaring and snarling, as the fight progressed just as his vision had forewarned. He jumped from Pyrra's back and ran towards the sound of battle. Godroi and Felspar were down on the ground locked in ferocious combat. He was sure, just as he had seen in his nightmares that it was to the death. Angus knew at once that he had to do something but what? He felt quite helpless as events unravelled beside him just as he had witnessed many times in the past few weeks. The two snarling dragons grappled and flipped each other as the snapped and clawed, trying to gain an advantage. Felspar managed to pull his hind legs in and with a ferocious roar pushed Godroi through the air, his body slamming against the stone wall of the church. Angus knew what was to happen next and he could see the same wound on Godroi's neck that he received at the start of the black dragon's surprise attack.

Ward Godroi had already warned Angus that Pyrra could not kill Felspar, but the golden dragon cried out in terrible agony from the wound he received in the unprovoked attack. Felspar had caught the golden dragon off-guard by calling out to him just as he was about to morph into his stained glass window and now Felspar stalked his prey in a semi-circle as he gloated at his handy work. The vile monster raised his claw in order to slash his victim in one final and fatal strike. Angus turned toward Pyrra, concern etched on his face and his whole body beseeching her to act. She realised what was about to happen and she slammed into the disbelieving black dragon, throwing him sideways. For a few seconds, Pyrra had given them the advantage as she engaged the now enraged Felspar with his back turned. Pyrra slashed at his hind leg with her tail as the foul creature attempted to rise from the ground sending him back to the earth in a crumpled heap. Godroi managed to stand upright and looked ready to take up the fight as he roared bravely and menacingly at the black dragon. Felspar, now realised he was outnumbered and was furious at his own single-mindedness of vision dulling his senses to Pyrra's approach.

"You can't guard him forever... I'll be back!" he vowed, as he took to the skies and swept up over the church.
Pyrra turned to see Godroi collapse forward, giving way to unconsciousness, as the pain from his wound became too much to bear.

Chapter 20

'Let Sleeping Dragon's Lie'

The younger Godroi wounded, dazed and stunned by the attack, was too weak to argue so he submitted to Pyrra and Angus' wish to escort him back to her lair to recuperate. First and foremost they had to hide Godroi from Felspar and set off for the sanctuary of Pyrra's cave. Pyrra kept a careful look out to ensure that they were not followed by the rogue dragon.

Whilst Godroi recovered in the safety of Pyrra's lair, Angus and Pyrra explained to him very patiently what had happened and that he was in grave danger from a dragon called Felspar.

"Ic don noht forstandan..." replied Godroi looking decidedly confused.

"Don't tell me he only speaks old English!" said Angus looking equally bewildered.

"It certainly sounds that way" she replied. "My old English is very rusty but I think he said he did not understand"

"So what do we do now?" asked Angus.

"Well I think it would be best if I speak to him in dragon as it will be much quicker" replied Pyrra.

Angus listened briefly, trying to get the gist as she started to explain everything in the dragon's own language. To him it sounded like a load of grunts, growls and small roars all jumbled together and certainly did not sound like a language. He decided to go and lie down for a while and left the two dragons speaking animatedly. Angus closed his eyes as he thought about the portal and how exciting but scary the whole thing was. It had been an interesting year and a half for Angus and thoughts of meeting Pyrra and her friends, flitted through his mind. He remembered Godroi's tale about the knight George and when he turned his thoughts to the Trials and Barfoot he realised he could make out some of the conversation the two dragons were having. Not all of it, but the odd word or growl made sense and he seemed to know what some of them meant. To Angus' surprise he was able to follow the conversation. Pyrra was explaining once again to Godroi what had happened and why they were there since the golden dragon was sceptical at first. The green dragon's gentle persuasion finally won him round, but since Godroi was too shocked to argue, he just slumped down wearily to the cave floor and closed his eyes.

"This ordeal has been too much for him and he must rest until his wounds heal a little more..." said Pyrra, "but I do not know what we can do about Felspar."

"I may have an idea about that, but we need to get back

home to Calmor!" stated Angus.

"That maybe so Angus, but we have not got enough Dragonore to get home!" replied Pyrra sadly.

"Barfoot has!" answered Angus smiling broadly.

"Of course... well done, we can get as much Dragonore as we need from Krubera, but I should explain to Godroi that he must not leave."

Pyrra told the sleepy dragon that they must leave him alone in the cave whilst they went to enlist further help. Without telling the wounded dragon where they were going, Angus and Pyrra made their way from the cave for Krubera to consult with the Guardian of the Cor Stan. In the timeframe they were currently in, this dragon was Godroi's predecessor; Ward Barfoot. They knew that they were now both targets of Felspar's wrath and bearing that in mind they used great stealth as they left.

Several hours later, the time travelling duo made the last leg of the now familiar journey to Krubera caves and the home of the Cor Stan. Angus was surprised to find the landscape exactly the same as it was in modern times. So much so, he had to stop and think for a moment as to which century he was actually in. The odd bit of scrub still gave relief to break the bleak rocky ground, and looking upwards, he saw the same view he was used to; nothing but foreboding rock as far as the eye could see. The entrance to the cave system was just as well hidden as in present time and it took them a moment to locate it.

As they made their way down into the cavern system it occurred to Angus that the Ward of the time, Barfoot, would already be in Great Hibernation.

"Pyrra, you'll probably have to wake Barfoot up" he said.

"I'm not very keen to do that…" she replied, "better to let sleeping dragon's lie" she added trying to make a joke worthy of Cyru.

The dragon could see that Angus was being deadly serious and in no mood for her attempted humour. She followed him through the cave system, which was a familiar path. They passed the mirror pool and turned into the cave room which contained the unique rock that was the source of the all dragons' magical powers. They reached the recumbent figure of the great wise Ward where he lay sleeping at the foot of the Cor Stan and Pyrra approached him reverently and tapped him gently with her fore claw. She spoke softly in dragon, close to his noble head and gradually the old dragon stirred.

He muttered something, aggrieved at the interruption, and was suddenly wide-awake and on his guard, at once mistrustful of the boy by the green dragon's side. Pyrra hastily explained in dragon who Angus was and began to tell the Ward how the boy would be responsible for reviving the Secret Society of Dragon Protectors some time in the future. Ward Barfoot visibly relaxed as he became more alert and awake. He studied Angus almost as if he recognised him. The white dragon heard their story and was sceptical at first, but once again Angus listened as Pyrra patiently explain everything to the wise old dragon.

When she had finished her story the Ward turned to Angus and looked at him thankfully.

"Halettan Draca Gast" said the old dragon.

Apart from 'hello' Angus was not sure what the rest meant but he was sure it was the same name the Barfoot in the future had used. He made a mental note to find out someday but for now they needed Dragonore. Pyrra looked at Angus curiously as if trying to figure something out. She racked her brains as she tried to recall the meaning of the words Barfoot had used to describe her young protector but, for the minute, it eluded her.

"Pyrra, have you asked him for the Dragonore?"

Interrupted from her contemplation, the green dragon asked Barfoot for a supply of the precious rock. Barfoot replied immediately and she turned to Angus again.

"He would like to know what you intend to do with it?"

At that point, Angus explained the idea he had hatched in his mind, but first they would have to go back to Calmor in their own present time to speak to Mrs T. The young protector was sure she would know just where to find the person whose help they needed. Pyrra again translated in dragon as Angus spoke and Ward Barfoot nodded in understanding. The Ward agreed to give them enough Dragonore to facilitate their journey back to the 21st century and enlist the help of the redoubtable Aurora Tek.

Chapter 21

'Plans and Arrangements'

Angus and Pyrra touched down at Calmor in the 21st century. Both of them were exhausted from the massive journey they had completed because not only had they travelled back from Krubera, they had traversed through time again. After they had spoken with Ward Barfoot he advised them to take great care when dealing with their adversary. He explained to Pyrra that she could not kill Felspar herself as it was not arweorðe. Pyrra told Angus afterwards that the word meant honourable and a dragon could not take the life of another dragon, either in anger, self defence nor even to save the life of another. Once they reached her lair they checked on Godroi and made sure he had stayed put. Only then did they travel back through the gateway. Angus marvelled at the experience as this time, knowing what to expect, he managed to keep his head raised and his eyes open. It was a magical experience and he drank it in right up until they passed through the pillars and the glare became so great he was forced to close his eyes.

Their reappearance in the field where the SSDP camped was almost instantaneous to the party that had seen them off.

Pyrra had concentrated on the point of time just after they had left the future and they arrived just as Rathlin was making his tea. Pyrra had followed Godroi's instruction very carefully so as not to arrive back prior to the time they had left. The Ward had laboured on about 'paradox's' and other such things that Angus had not really understood, but his point had been made and they kept strictly to his rules. Rathlin had been so shocked to see them he nearly dropped his tea and when Angus told him the plan he got very excited and dropped the mug anyway.

Having flown to Calmor, they now stood wearily at the rear of the castle where Caedmon positively bounded over to greet them. This confounded them greatly as, once again he seemed completely out of character and it was as if their last meeting had not happened.

"My friends how are you?" he called to them.

He seemed to have forgotten seeing them only a few days previously when he had been totally offhand and exceedingly unfriendly.

"We're… fine!" replied Pyrra cautiously. "How are you feeling now?"

"Why I'm fine… never been better!" replied the grey dragon happily.

"But you weren't the last time we met!" said Pyrra eyeing

Caedmon warily.

"Wasn't I? Well that's strange are you sure it was me?"

"Yes of course it was you… four of us visited you at your Quinton House gatepost…"

"Gatepost? I've not used that for many years now…" interrupted the grey dragon, "I live at Quinton House but I hide in a statue in the grounds… nowhere near the gate!"

Angus left an exhausted and now confused Pyrra, politely arguing with the baffling grey dragon. He rationalised that Caedmon was suffering from some kind of short-term memory loss as a result of awakening from the Great Hibernation. He quickly put it out of his own mind and went into the castle alone in search of Mrs T.

The somnolent lad trudged into the kitchen and called Mrs T's name but received no answer. He forced his weary limbs to carry him into the Great Hall and was told by another protector that she was in the Turret Room. He tramped up the stairs feeling nauseous from lack of sleep, as he went slowly past he glanced at the paintings of dragons found. He now recognised most of them, even the half a dozen new finds since the Trials. As he turned into the west wing he stopped suddenly and turned back. At first he thought it was his tired mind playing a trick on him, but sure enough there it was, as plain as day. He walked from one painting to the other and then smiled. It was simple really and he would need to do a little more investigation work on it, but he was content that he had solved that little conundrum which he and Pyrra would need to deal with later.

Finding Mrs T in the Turret Room at last, Angus explained their predicament. They did not know exactly when Felspar was planning to attack Godroi but it was clear that Pyrra would not be able to kill the black dragon.

"So you see we need some help!" he finished.
Angus heard a tapping sound coming from behind the filing cabinet and was surprised to see Meredith Quinton-Jones as she flicked through some of the older files already alphabetically arranged.

"It's okay to discuss things but let's keep it down" whispered Mrs T to Angus.
Once they were seated at the table on the other side of the room Mrs T confessed.

"She's a diligent worker, and Rathlin says, an important and trusted member of the team…" she said quietly looking over her shoulder towards the dark haired woman, who for her part seemed oblivious to the conversation they were having, or that Angus was even there. "She has certainly spent a lot of time here… but based on what you said to Rathlin, I'm still not sure I trust her!"

Angus recovered his train of thought when Mrs T asked him what his idea was and the lad eagerly divulged his plan.

"Okay, like I said we need help and I was thinking, with the portal, we could get anybody we want!" he said enthusiastically, his tiredness forgotten for the time-being.

"Sounds interesting…" she whispered, "Go on."

"I want to find George!" stated Angus, "he's the first ever dragon protector and he's not bound by any dragon code of arweorðe… or whatever it's called. He would surely help Godroi."

Angus though the knight was the key; in fact he felt sure of it.

"That sounds like an extremely good idea" she replied smiling warmly. "So what can I do to help?" she asked frowning slightly.

"I need you to pinpoint exactly where, and when, we can find him!" replied Angus seriously.

Mrs T looked thoughtful at this request, what Angus asked was very tricky indeed. To try and pinpoint where they might encounter the Knight George at any given time in history was extremely difficult. So much folklore and tales of the knight's deeds were either made up or distorted nonsense, it would be difficult to sift through the whole lot.

While the conversation had been going on Meredith moved across the room towards them and offered her assistance.

"Do you need any help finding something?" she gushed.

"No dear, we're fine thank you!" replied Mrs T as she graciously declined Meredith's offer.

"Well if you do just shout… I think I'm beginning to know my way around now and it's all very interesting. I can see why you like it up here!" Meredith smiled.

Mrs T watched the woman go back to the filing cabinet and Angus struggled to recognise any emotion on her face. One thing he was sure of though, Mrs T did not like the dark haired woman and certainly did not trust her.

The ex-librarian's face suddenly beamed as her smile lit it up; she enjoyed nothing better than a challenge, especially a historical one. She set to work at once using the vast resources of the SSDP headquarters, and sifted through many conflicting myths and legends that threw up vague dates. She began to sense the boy's frustration and sent him over to Dermot in the lighthouse to check a few things with Godroi via the satellite link. She wanted to know approximately what age George was when the dragon first met him and anything that would be a clue as to his whereabouts. That was the time when Godroi charmed the knight sufficiently so that the man did not kill him, as he had been ordered to do. Instead they became great friends and the knight had helped Godroi find a cave to live in quite secretly and peacefully.

Meredith followed Angus and chatted amiably to him all the way across the lawn towards the lighthouse. Dermot welcomed them in his normal exuberant fashion by offering refreshments and making his guests comfortable. Meredith asked questions about the exciting journey Angus and Pyrra had taken and on how they managed to save Godroi.

"He's not saved yet…" replied Angus, "We still have to stop Felspar!"

"And am sure you'll be finding a way lad!" said Dermot laughing. "You always seem to manage somehow!" he added causing Angus to redden.

Angus left the small couch and switched on the sat-link allowing it to whirr into life and connect with its opposite terminal in Krubera.

The young protector openly explained his adventure once again to Godroi and how he planned to defeat Felspar. The Ward and Finian were seriously impressed with the idea and the Ward gave him all the information he could, as to the best period in time to encounter the legendary knight. Having written down all that he needed, Angus said goodbye and flicked off the terminal. He could hardly keep his eyes open now and even the excitement of his proposed expedition to locate George was barely enough to keep him going.

"You poor dear... you're exhausted" said Meredith taking his shoulders as they returned to the castle. "Let me take your message to Aurora and you go for a lie down" she suggested.

"No I'm fine... I want to do it... then I'll rest" replied Angus irritably.

Meredith smiled sweetly and indicated towards the castle with her palm open, allowing Angus to lead the way.

Mrs T frowned as she had just heard the news that George was a young man who had just won his knightly spurs when he and Godroi met. She continued to search based on the dates Godroi had provided and finally pinpointed March 798 as a good place in history to find him.

"You see, in this particular year George was sent to Paris by the Wessex King Brihtric to enlist the help of the Mercian King Offa in raising an army against the Viking invaders. This was a dangerous trip as a Thegn travelling alone would be a prime target for anyone intent on sacking the country" explained Mrs T.

"What's a Thegn?" asked Angus.

"It's what they called a knight back then, basically a bodyguard to the king" she replied.

Meredith began drumming her nails on the desk and Mrs T shot her an irritated look.

"Do go and put the kettle on Meredith, there's a dear. I'm parched and would kill for a cup of Earl Grey" she asked politely.

When the woman left the room and the drumming ceased, Mrs T confided to Angus.

"I'm sure she's a good egg, at least Rathlin seems to think so, but her mannerisms do annoy me… must she drum those nails all the time on every surface she touches?" she said frowning.

Angus just smiled at her childish annoyance and seeing this, Mrs T returned his smile and refocused on the plan.

"Let me get this straight… that's about 500 years earlier than we need him" then sharing his thoughts aloud, "but with Dragonore George can travel in time with us to the 13th century on a special mission for the SSDP… and since he is not a dragon, it's possible to travel into the future because he's with us and we know that future!" finished Angus proud of his reasoning.

Rathlin had just arrived at Calmor as he was eager to find out what was going on and had just entered the room and heard this comment.

"You're right lad, it is forbidden for dragons to travel into an unknown future, but since you'll be going no further than today it would be allowed… by Jove I think you've struck gold with your plan!" he said as he slapped the boy hard on the back nearly knocking him over in his enthusiasm.

They discussed the finer points and Rathlin confirmed that they had enough Dragonore to make another trip back in time.

"By the way Aurora, I have mislaid a couple of files I was working on the other day and I've turned this room upside down but can't find them anywhere… have you been moving things around?" said Rathlin, once the arrangements were fully understood.

"No dear… but it's funny you should say that as I seem to have lost a couple of dragon artefacts I was intending to send for carbon dating… I was going to ask you the same question" she replied, puzzled.

They turned at a noise from the doorway and Meredith was returning with a tea pot and cups which she had managed to bash against the door almost tipping the tray over.

"Are you all right with that Meredith?" said Rathlin.

"How clumsy of me… I'm sorry if I interrupted something,

don't mind me" she replied looking embarrassed.

"I was assuming that I had merely misplaced them… but if it's happened to you too…" Mrs T glanced at Meredith for a second, "well… it's probably nothing. Just us two getting forgetful in our old age!" she finished.

"You're not that old!" laughed Angus who had seen the direction of her look.

"Don't worry about it just now… Tracking down George is far more exciting… anyway, tell me, what it was like going through the portal?" asked Rathlin enthusiastically.

Angus went into a lengthy explanation about travel through the portal and what they encountered on the other side.

"Ah thank you dear" Mrs T addressed Meredith with a big smile as she handed her a cup of tea.

'Hmmm pity no biscuits' thought Angus and he launched into an account of the medieval fair and how Pyrra was attacked by angry peasants bearing pitchforks, which made everyone laugh. Rathlin was particularly interested in the battle with Felspar and insisted Angus spare no details; until the lad could not speak for yawning.

"When was the last time you slept Angus?" asked Mrs T.

"Uhhhhh" Angus yawned again, "I don't know… Friday night I guess" he managed to reply.

"Yes and since you've also spent a day in the past you must be exhausted" she replied in a motherly tone, "Okay off to bed now and get some sleep!"

"But…" Angus began to reply, trying to convince her of the urgency of the situation.

"No buts… it's time travel, so you can arrive and leave whenever you want and never be late" said Mrs T cutting him off while she ushered him to his room.

"No point in arguing lad" laughed Rathlin.

Soon Angus was tucked up in the four poster bed and knowing Pyrra was recuperating in the Blue Dragon Fire plants that surrounded the castle, he dreamt of meeting George the knight, the first member of The Secret Society of Dragon Protectors.

Chapter 22

'The Dragon Slayer'

Angus awoke to find daylight streaming through the mullioned windows. He got dressed and ate quickly as he was keen to find Pyrra and get going. Aurora Tek waved him off as he and Pyrra made their way back to Wellshire and the portal with Rathlin and Cyru flying escort. The band of protectors and dragons still waited at the tents, pitched not too far from the tall stone pillars that marked the gateway. Rathlin presented Pyrra with more Dragonore and once again she made the now familiar transition through time; only on this occasion they aimed at March the 16th, 798.

The village of Stanbury appeared before Angus and Pyrra, just as it had before. As the bright purple light faded Angus could see that the village was much smaller than on their last visit. He surmised that the village started as only one or two farms growing to a hamlet as families increased and more people moved to that area. Pyrra wasted no time in setting off before any of the villagers noticed their presence, but she did not bother to go to her lair for more Dragonore. She explained to Angus that her cave did not have any spare pieces of the mineral hidden there yet and that since she was probably there now it may not be a good idea to bump into her younger self.

Pyrra flew into the cloud cover to keep from being detected by anyone on the ground and with Angus calling out from his notes; they managed to navigate towards the area Mrs T believed George would be found in. Taking a chance, they landed in a small empty pasture and dismounting Angus ran to a small cart track they had noticed from the air. The track led to a cross roads and two villages could be found along the length of two of the tracks leading east and west. The southerly track led towards the sea through a valley and it was then that Angus first spotted them. Mrs T had warned Angus about this and he never expected to run into any, but sure enough he watched as the long line of armed men progressed quickly through the valley.

"Pyrra get back into the trees, the Vikings are coming!" he called to his green scaly friend.

She did as she was told and was deeply concerned when she realised Angus had not joined her. Instead the strong-willed lad had positioned himself nearer the track in order to get a better look at the invaders.

At first he could only make out a long line of men moving very quickly and stealthily along the rutted track, but as they drew nearer he began to see more and more detail. Angus

marvelled at the sight before him and he wished he had
brought a camera. Every warrior bore a round shield made of

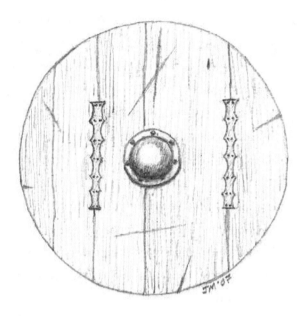

wood which was decorated in simple colours and had either a
central spike or metal ball in the middle. They all carried spears
with long thin blades on the top, giving them a very deadly look
indeed. Each man had a helmet but it was not as Angus had
imagined they would be. He always thought of Vikings wearing
horns or wings, but in actual fact they were simple steel
helmets that moulded round the head. The helmet was held

fast with what looked like rivets and all had a piece fashioned so that it extended over the eyes or nose of the wearer. They wore simple tunics that covered a short mail shirt and the belts they had served to carry the long swords hanging from their waists. Some of them carried rope and others, axes over shoulders, or on backs. All of them looked very serious and alert. He could imagine that being in a foreign region where you attempted to steal and plunder from the locals, would make you very wary indeed. He watched as the foremost Viking stopped at the crossroads and stooped to look at the ground. He was the largest of the men and Angus assumed he was the leader. His dirty blond beard was pleated under his chin and his long straggly hair flowed ungainly from under his helmet. The man studied the tracks and footprints on the ground and then pointing along the north track he set off with his band of warriors following on behind him.

Angus knelt behind the fallen trees and undergrowth he had chosen as his viewing point and watched them almost jog out of sight as quickly as they had appeared.

"Seen enough you young rascal?" asked Pyrra right behind his ear and causing him to almost jump the log in front of him.

"Yeah… sorry Pyrra…" he answered gauchely, "It's just they were so cool and I really couldn't resist a look!" he added in token explanation.

"I'm afraid you would not think so if they ever caught you!" replied Pyrra seriously. "But never mind that… where is George?"

"He should be here but maybe we are too early… perhaps he still has to come down the northern track" suggested Angus. They decided to travel further up the rutted trail and see if the could intercept the knight they sought.

The pair had flown for about ten minutes when they saw what looked like a large house with stables at the rear. Some carts stood outside, a few of which had horses tethered and recognising the sign outside he called to Pyrra to land nearby.

"It's the Blue Dragon!" said Angus as touched down.

"What, Cyru's blue dragon pub?" Pyrra asked.

"Yeah… do you think Cyru will be there?"

"I doubt it as he was too young to be on his own at this time" replied Pyrra thoughtfully.

"It's a pity my Dragonore is burnt out as it would make it easier to find George!" said Angus dejectedly.

"Angus you need to remember that he will only speak Old English and you will not be able to understand each other… This is going to be tricky but first you need to find out if he is there!" warned Pyrra with a serious look on her face.

The bold lad walked towards the coach house taking in the atmosphere of the scene before him. Chickens and pigs roamed around the road getting in the way of all manner of people. Some of them looked suspiciously at Angus as he passed, eyeing up his strange attire with a look of mistrust on their dirty faces. Most of them seemed too busy, packing their carts with belongings and Angus watched as they set off along the track in the opposite direction from the Vikings. Upon reaching the door of the Inn, Angus heard a commotion from within. A group of men were discussing something in a very animated fashion and all seemed to be directing their efforts towards a tall man dressed in a chain-linked shirt, similar to the Vikings, but longer in the body. They all stopped talking and turned to the doorway when they heard it open, some of the men stood with toothless mouths gaping at the sight of the stranger. Angus could see the tallest man was a warrior, and along with the sword that hung from his side he had a long tear-shaped shield. The shield leant against the table beside the knight and Angus knew from the emblem on it that he had found the person he was looking for. It was a large golden dragon emblazoned on a red background.

The young protector walked up to George and saw that he wore his Dragonore around his neck. This confirmed to Angus that he had the correct man but now he had to convince the knight to follow him to Pyrra so she could converse with him in Old English. That would be tricky. He racked his brains for anything that could help him while the men still stared at the weird boy who had interrupted their plea for George to tackle the approaching Vikings.

"Halettan George!" Angus said awkwardly. Then he pointed to the Dragonore around the knight's neck. "Godroi!" Angus finished by motioning that the stunned man should follow him outside. George looked at Angus for a second before taking his Dragonore in his hand and staring at it for a few moments.

"Eow cunnan Godroi?" asked the knight looking up at Angus.

The lad could only guess at what was said and nodding his head he again bade George to follow him. The thegn turned to the men around him saying something Angus could not understand and judging by their reactions, they were not happy about this decision. They gestured towards Angus as they babbled in a coarse dialect but George waved off their remonstrations and followed Angus from the Inn.

The knight called to Angus and motioned towards the back of the Inn where the horses were stabled. Angus nodded his understanding and George left the lad waiting among the stream of people as they continued to take flight. The bearded and chainmail clad man reappeared, leading a large white horse that stood proudly beside its master whilst it carried his many weapons and shield. He indicated that Angus should lead the way and having satisfied himself that this heavily armoured man was indeed a dragon protector and the man they needed, Angus took him to meet Pyrra. Angus' caution was wise because, if he had got the wrong man, the knight might actually turn dragon slayer and run his scaly friend through the moment they met. As it turned out he need not have worried as George instantly recognised the green dragon as being an old friend of Godroi's.

"Halettan Pyrra" cried the man as he walked forward to greet her by pulling his sword from its sheath and holding it flat and vertical to his forehead.

Pyrra replied in what Angus thought was Old English but George looked at her strangely as if he had struggled to understand. The pair conversed for a while and Angus realised this might take some time.

"Did you tell him about the Vikings Pyrra?" he asked impatiently.

"I'm getting to that… he was a bit confused at first as my

Anglo-Saxon is a bit rusty but I've explained about being from the future and although he is sceptical he is willing to help… but he needs to fight off the Vikings first!"

"Where's his army then?" asked Angus looking around.

"He doesn't have one and he told me the villagers are too scared to help him!" replied Pyrra looking doubtful about their chances.

The dragon turned to speak to George once more and Angus looked down the track as it meandered down the slope and through a forest at the bottom. His mind was working overtime and he pictured a scene in his head.

"Pyrra… I've got an idea!" shouted Angus excitedly. He quickly explained what he had in mind and Pyrra in turn enlightened George. The knight smiled as he understood the plan, and he walked over to Angus and placed his hand on the young protector's shoulder.

"Min beadurinc geong, freond!" he said.

Pyrra translated what was said and Angus grinned up into the strong and bearded face of the great knight and thought 'Me, his young warrior… Cool!'

The trio prepared themselves to enact their plan as the Viking warband marched through the trees. Pyrra took off and sped over the forest roaring loudly to alert the invaders to her presence. She spotted them on the track, diving between the gaps in the forest, cut by the track as she sprayed flames in every direction. The Vikings scattered into the trees running for cover and some of them managed to throw spears that missed their mark by some distance, such was the speed and suddenness of the attack. Angus could hear the men holler and shout to each other as they tried to regroup and defend themselves from this ferocious and terrifying beast. Pyrra made one more pass, but not as low as the first one as the men were ready for her now. Angus watched as arrows flew out of the trees and zipped past Pyrra's body; he fervently hoped she would not get hurt.

Pyrra landed lightly in front of the knight as he stood on the crest of the hillside. Playing her part well, she roared another challenge to George with her back to the trees. Some of the peasants tentatively appeared from the track that led from the Inn, curious about the strange noises coming from the direction of the forest. Angus could see the Vikings as they began to creep to the edge of the wood, their reluctance to move from the cover of the trees openly apparent. He gave the signal to Pyrra and she reared menacingly before George who stood resolutely, his long dragon emblazoned shield in one hand and his sword in the other. Beneath his silver helmet Angus could see the stern look on the man's face as he challenged the fierce dragon for all to see.

Pyrra moved forward and swung her tail viciously at the knight who in turn blocked the blow with his bodyweight behind his shield. The swipe did not harm him but it was still powerful enough to rock him backwards a few steps. She quickly rounded on him again, but not too fast, and spat a bout of flame at his unprotected side. At first Angus thought she would burn the knight but with catlike reflexes he ducked and rolled in one movement, avoiding the deadly fire. Seeing her chance Pyrra went in for the kill as more peasants arrived to witness their hero doing battle with a deadly beast, and thrusting her neck forward she attempted to bite the man while he crouched on the ground. George brought up his shield and Pyrra's nose battered off its steel surface and appeared to daze her. The knight quickly stood and used the hilt of his sword as he thrust it into the side of her head. Everyone saw the green dragon roar angrily as she began to circle the knight looking for the killer blow. When the angle was correct and everyone could see from the track behind and the trees, the combatants lunged at each other in one final and dramatic scream of glory!

Angus shut his eyes unable to watch his best friend killed before him. The silence that followed was surreal as Angus could only hear the wind in the trees where the Vikings remained hidden. A cheer rang up from the peasants as they realised that the Thegn, George the dragon slayer had defeated another monster in mortal combat. Angus opened his eyes to see the triumphant knight pull his sword from the body of the beast at his feet, making him panic until George surreptitiously winked at him. Pyrra's body slumped over and rolled down the hill slightly scraping the grass and revealing the chalky ground below. The great knight roared his victory to the heavens and turned to the forest with his sword and shield held high above his head.

"Becuman duguð ond byrigan min iren!" he bellowed threateningly.

At this the peasants cheered and bringing what weapons they had ran to the crest of the hill and began their own war chant in the name of their hero George.

Stunned by what he had just witnessed, Angus stared in disbelief as the leader of the Vikings walked from the trees and stood at the base of the hill. The tall blond haired man removed his helmet and placing it on his chest, he bowed to George who stood resolutely atop the hill; the invaders respect for his enemy clear in his eyes for all to see. The Viking warrior replaced his helmet and at a signal from him the others in his warband retreated into the forest never to be seen again. As

the leader returned to the trees the peasants cheered with great delight at the astonishing victory George had materialised from nothing. The hero of the day led the people back to the Inn and made it clear to all not to desecrate the body of the dragon, leaving his new squire to guard it.

Angus watched the victorious party march off back to the tavern, the knight lifted onto the shoulders of the jubilant people in celebration.

"Are they gone yet?" whispered Pyrra from the side of her mouth.

"Yeah I think it's safe… we can go now" replied Angus smiling.

"I'm glad they fell for it!" she said as she opened her eyes and stretched her rear legs.

"Are you kidding… it was awesome!" he cried excitedly. "I almost believed it myself!"

As Pyrra got up from the grassy slope she clawed at the ground revealing yet more of the chalky soil below. Angus looked at the pattern she had accidentally formed on the ground and realised where they were.

"Pyrra this is Serpent Tor!" he said looking flabbergasted. "You created Serpent Tor and it was in my dreams!"

"No I didn't!" replied the confused dragon.

"Yes you did... at least you have now… somehow my dreams are coming true!" shouted the lad breathlessly.

"I don't think they are just dreams Angus!" replied Pyrra as the young protector jumped onto her back.

"What do you mean?" he asked confused.

"I think they are messages Angus, but from whom I don't know…" she replied looking round at his thoughtful and troubled expression, "This conversation can wait for another time. We have work to do and a rendezvous with a knight to keep!"

With that she sprang into the darkening dusk, keeping out of sight of the local population.

Chapter 23

'Ultimate Battle'

Before meeting George, Angus and Pyrra flew back to Krubera for more Dragonore and the experience of re-awakening Ward Barfoot felt very strange. To Angus it was like déjà-vu as they had already done so before in exactly the same fashion. The whole thing confused him as this was actually the first time he had met Barfoot, and the next time centuries from now, would be the second time, but that had already happened. His head hurt at the thought of it all and he decided the best approach was just to get on with the job at hand, saving Godroi, and keeping the present as he and Pyrra knew it to be.

George arrived at the portal on foot having left his trusty steed at the stables and carrying his sheathed sword, a spear and his striking shield. After a brief discussion in Old English the knight jumped up behind Angus and they took off from their hiding place to head for the portal. Pyrra struggled with the extra weight of the fully armoured knight and it occurred to Angus that their progress would be very slow and Pyrra would soon be tired. The passage through the gateway was troublesome and at first Angus thought his friend would not be able to attain the speed required to propel them into the future. However, his fears were unfounded as she managed to gain height and dropping from a higher altitude allowed her to fly faster into the portal. The knight held Angus tightly and shouted some sort of curse in Old English as the purple light enveloped them. The larger version of the village of Stanbury appeared before them and Pyrra wasted no time in putting some distance between herself and its inhabitants. She did not get far before she had to stop and rest; the weight of the additional passenger was just too great for her to sustain any longer.

Angus and George waited for her to recuperate and Angus knew they were vulnerable out in the open with no Dragonore to grant Pyrra invisibility.

"I'll be okay in a few minutes Angus… Don't worry" said the tired dragon, not wanting to hold them up.
Angus did not say anything to her but patted her reassuringly.

Something caught his attention, and shielding his eyes he peered into the sky. A stone grey dragon travelling in the same direction they needed to go in; seemed to be making great headway. Angus knew at once that it was Caedmon and he bellowed as loud as he could to attract the dragon's attention.

"I will go and get him Angus, in case he is in one of his bad moods!" said Pyrra, bravely trying to appear stronger than she actually felt.

"No Pyrra, I want to see which one it is!" replied Angus mysteriously.

"What do you mean *which one*?" asked Pyrra confused.

"There are two of them!" answered Angus smugly. "I found out in Calmor and I forgot to tell you about it… they must be twins or something, but there are two. Rathlin has two paintings of stone grey dragons, and they are identical!"

"But why didn't Rathlin say so?" she frowned.

"My guess is he didn't realise, but it's all there on the wall… one in a garden statue and one on a gate!" he replied as he watched the dragon make a turn and head in their direction. The trouble was they could not easily distinguish between the good one and the more devious one until they actually spoke to them.

Caedmon landed heavily beside Pyrra and at first Angus thought it was the nasty twin by the way the grey dragon looked at the humans. However he realised that the dragon probably did not trust any humans at this time, especially one armoured for battle. Pyrra, in dragon, explained to Caedmon who everybody was and asked him if he would be willing to help them. She knew that the gate dragon would say no or utter some other negative comment, but she was glad to hear that he was only too glad to help. She asked him if he had seen Felspar and he told her that he had not, but that he had just visited his twin at the gatepost.

"He says that he's just returning to Paris and that his twin, who is also called Caedmon for some strange reason, has spoken to Felspar!" she translated.

Angus pondered this information, as Pyrra explained to Caedmon where they were going and what they needed him to do. After a few minutes Angus was seated on Pyrra's back as they waited for George to climb onto Caedmon's.

"Are you sure he's the good one?" whispered Angus.

"As sure as I can be, but I think I will ask him to wait with George on the other side of the mountain, while I take you to the lair first" she replied, just before taking off.

Upon entering the cave, George, dropped to one knee and embraced his old friend Godroi. Angus and Pyrra left them alone to catch up, as it was quite an emotional moment and they felt awkward witnessing the rekindling of a very old and special friendship between man and dragon. Pyrra went out from the cave to find Caedmon where she had left him and to thank him for giving George a ride. She still had some slight doubts as to which of the twins he may be and wanted to make sure he did return to France and not reveal their whereabouts to Felspar. Pyrra kept her fears to herself, calling Angus and rejoining George and Godroi.

The four stayed within the warmth of Pyrra's cave until she had recovered from her exertions. The heat from the rock in the centre of the cave was revived time and again as they discussed in Old English the staged 'killing of the dragon' that drove off the Vikings. Angus struggled to keep up with the conversation but it was obvious from the translations, and the manner in which George addressed him, that the knight was very pleased with his new dragon protecting friend.

"Godroi wants to know what the plan is to stop Felspar and to be honest, I don't even know how we can find him" she said.

"We can flush him into the open…" said Angus thoughtfully, "I've been thinking about this since I knew about the Caedmon twins and meeting the good one tonight convinced me it will work" added Angus furtively.

"How does that help?" asked Pyrra.

"We can use Godroi as bait and if we happen to tell the gatepost Caedmon that he will be using the portal after visiting Marnham Church to get some Dragonore…"

"Ah I see where you're going with it…" she interrupted, "very clever Angus… I will translate this for them" she added turning to the others.

Soon they had formulated a plan, which they quickly put into action, with Pyrra visiting the wicked Caedmon at the dragon gatepost where he was hibernating. The next stage involved Godroi flying over Marnham Church as bait to draw Felspar out from wherever he was hiding. The plan was to lure him towards the portal at Stanbury where Angus, Pyrra and George waited. George would then finally become a dragon slayer to save his old friend and unbeknown to both of them, save the dragon who would become the future Ward.

As is usually the case, the best-laid plans never come off exactly as intended, and this one was no exception. As Godroi flew around the church and circled deliberately visible overhead, the terrified villagers soon became very angry at yet another terrifying beast appearing near their village. Quickly they organised and armed themselves intent on driving off the colour-changing dragon that had plagued their lives of late. Godroi received the same welcome that Pyrra had previously enjoyed but unlike her, Godroi managed a hearty roar which sent the peasants scattering in all directions!

At last a black speck appeared on the horizon as Felspar approached his quarry at great speed. Godroi immediately sped towards Stanbury which made the peasants believe he was about to attack the village. Felspar knew something was afoot as Caedmon had pre-warned him and although he did not know exactly what or who awaited him, he eagerly homed in on his golden prey. From their hiding place near the village Angus watched the approaching black shadow as it rapidly caught up with the still injured Godroi. Angus wanted to shout out a warning, but dared not give away their presence just yet. They needed Godroi to draw the attacker nearer to the portal so that they could use the village buildings to hem him in.

Godroi sensed Felspar was near as he landed and he anxiously waited for his opponent's next move. The golden dragon flinched slightly from the pain of his recent battle scars leaving Angus in torment as he felt helpless to intervene. Suddenly a black shadow fell over the golden dragon as Felspar spiralled from the air and landed with a resounding thud within feet of his prey. The black dragon drew himself up to his full and impressive height and began to taunt Godroi. By comparison the golden dragon seemed to shrink in stature as Felspar baring angry teeth, stalked his pray.

"You should have stayed hidden Godroi…" he snarled, "Now I can finish you once and for all!"

With that, he leapt forward and bowled over Godroi with a mighty push; his slashing claws reopening the wound and causing Godroi to howl in pain. The malicious beast loomed over the stricken body of Godroi and raised his claw for the killer blow. Angus had seen this many times in his dreams of late.

"Now!" shouted Angus, as he pushed the battle-ready knight out from his hiding place and into the fray.

Felspar spun round in surprise just as Pyrra hit him from behind in a tackle that sent him away from Godroi and into the centre of the village.

The black dragon growled menacingly as he rolled over, righting his body slowly, as if the knight that stood before him posed no threat to him at all.

"Is this the best you can do Pyrra?" he taunted. "A boy, a crippled dragon, a frightened man and you... My, my I am so disappointed!"

Pyrra did not answer and instead attempted to help Godroi to his feet so she could move him to a safer spot.

"Don't go too far Pyrra... I'll be back for you!" Felspar sneered as he turned slowly to face the knight.

Angus braced himself for what was about to happen, as he saw the black dragon coil his muscular body ready to strike the initial blow. The great Knight George stood stock still with no sign of emotion on his face and waited for his foe to make the first move. Felspar sprung forward and snapped his jaws in midair just where George had stood only a split second before. The knight had anticipated the attack and deftly rounded on the dragon with a stab of his spear into his shoulder. The beast growled and grabbed the weapon in the middle of the shaft, snapping it in the process. Angus could see that the wound was not deep, and once again, Felspar circled the knight looking for an opening. George kept his shield close to his chainmail covered body and the concentration in his eyes reflected the life and death situation he was now in. Felspar took a deep breath and spat a jet of flame at the knight that engulfed him and set fire to one of the buildings behind. Angus watched in horror as the flame continued to pour from the black dragon's mouth and he feared that George would surely perish. Finally the fire ceased and Angus could still see no sign of the tall man. Suddenly, from the smoke-filled area of the village, stepped the knight with his sword drawn and his head held high. George switched into fighting overdrive as he cut and thrust with his heavy sword, wielding it above his head like a cleaver. The black dragon parried and repelled every blow and in turn he retaliated with all the ferocious power he possessed only to be countered skilfully every time. George swung a mighty blow and slashed the black dragon's chest, sending him reeling. Angus watched him take a step forward as Felspar spat more flames at his prey. Once again George dodged the attack as fire engulfed yet another home within the village.

The peasants had watched in terror, as not one but three dragons appeared from nowhere and began to destroy the hamlet they had built over the years. Terrified, they abandoned their homes and scattered into the countryside, never to return to the cursed place of dragons.

Angus was forced to move as the wind blew flames onto the other wooden huts, which, unchecked took hold and began to devour the timber. He took up a position near the portal and used one of the pillars as a secure place from which to view the battle. Felspar sensed he was beginning to lose the upper hand and he could see the man before him grow in confidence. Again the dragon lunged at the knight without warning, only to be thwarted by the sturdy shield that now showed the ravages of the battle on its outer skin. George swung his arm in a massive arc building up speed and power as he slashed into the skin of Felspar's shoulder to bite into flesh and bone. The black dragon howled in rage and pain as he limped backwards to avoid the searing blade of this would-be dragon slayer, only to be caught once more as the knight sprang forward and thrust the blade into his unprotected flank.

Felspar fell to the ground and Angus could see his eyes flicker as the pain from the wounds rendered him unconscious. George sensed victory in the offing, and the well-trained knight moved in to finish off his quarry, stepping forward with less caution to make the final blow. He placed his shield down and taking his sword in both hands hefted it high above his head, point downwards, to thrust it through the dragons head. 'We've won' thought Angus as the blade glinted in the sunshine, but George suddenly span into the air in a trajectory that saw him land hard against the other pillar of the portal. Angus watched in dismay as the knight's limp body slumped to the ground, apparently lifeless. Although clearly wounded, Felspar had feigned weakness, and once he had caught the knight off guard, he had used his great black spiked tail to sweep George clean off his feet. Angus called to George but the knight was rendered unconscious from the blow, and the boy felt a rising panic as he saw the enraged black dragon stand up looking around in search of Godroi.

Pyrra meanwhile, had made good use of the distraction the battle had provided and had moved Godroi out of sight but still not far enough to be completely safe. She had no idea that the battle had taken a nasty turn for the worse and the green dragon grew worried at the silence. She peered round the barrow that hid Godroi, but by the time she decided to take a chance and risk a proper look at what had happened, Felspar was already bearing down on the unresponsive knight.

"Leave him!" she snarled.

The black dragon stopped and turned his head to Pyrra.

"So you've decided to come out of hiding then... You can't win... I'm too strong and now this pest of a human is dealt with I will move onto Godroi and there is nothing you can do about it!" he replied, as he stamped on George's sword and snapped it in two.

"It is strange how we came to be here isn't it..." Felspar sneered, "I never knew time travel was possible until I touched Godroi that day at the Trials!"

"What are you talking about?" snarled Pyrra.

"It was Godroi who passed me the knowledge of the portal..." he laughed in reply, "When I attacked him at the end of the transference a little of the knowledge he received came to me! It's ironic that it will be his eventual undoing!" he boasted.

Pyrra made a move to silence the foul beast before her.

"Now, now... remember the code Pyrra!" laughed Felspar.

The black dragon turned to look at the recumbent knight and Angus could see he was unable to defend himself as Felspar moved in for the kill. Angus could see the look of evil in the red eyes of the black dragon just before the roar of Pyrra's charge turned the dragon's head away.

Instinctively Angus ran forward and grabbed the hilt of the knight's broken sword, which he could barely lift. Using a superhuman strength he had no idea he possessed, he lifted the broken and unwieldy sword and staggered towards Felspar who turned as Angus bellowed in fury and frustration similar to the incident with the bullies. The dragon laughed at Angus as he knew that a small human child did not possess the strength to even wound him. But somehow Angus moved into dragon time and this burst of speed, caught Felspar off guard and created enough force to get through his thick hide. Angus focused all his energy and thrusting upwards with the sword he managed to pierce the rogue dragon right through his heart stone. The blow broke the precious stone in half and the heavy blade entered the exposed weaker underside of the dragon's body and deep into his chest. Reality struck the black beast as he screamed in an agony he had never experienced before. He slapped Angus across the chest with a fore claw and sent the young protector reeling backwards onto the grass. Felspar clutched the hilt of the sword and shrieked again as he pulled the half blade from his own body; blood rapidly coursing from the wound. Angus, dazed and bruised, watched as the stricken dragon staggered off, stumbling from side to side. Angus was stunned by the enormity of what he had done and once again could not believe, nor understand, the powers he had managed to call upon.

Chapter 24

'A Knights Honour'

Pyrra ignored Felspar in her concern for her protector, convinced that he was fatally wounded by the blow. However the irrepressible lad sat up and rubbed his chest, frowning and seemingly unharmed.

"Are you okay?" she asked.

"I'm fine Pyrra… a little sore, but he didn't hit me that hard" replied Angus staunchly.

"That was a very brave thing to do…" she said causing Angus to grin, "but it was also extremely stupid!" The lad just carried on grinning and nodding in acknowledgement of her comments, too sore to argue he picked himself up from the ground. Pyrra wanted to discuss what had just transpired before her eyes. For the first time ever, she had witnessed a human using the same powers a dragon gained from Dragonore, but it would have to wait, as more pressing matters needed her attention.

"I hope George is okay!" he said concerned. "What about Godroi?"

"Godroi is fine and will heal, but we need to get out of here quickly, just in case the villagers come back!" she replied. "I will

get Godroi and you see if you can revive our knight."
Angus did as he was told and staggered over to check on
George. The knight's helm was dented on one side where it
had hit the stone pillar. Angus removed it carefully, and taking
off his backpack, found a bandage he had for emergencies and
began to tend a nasty wound on the knight's sword arm. As he
watched over the still unconscious man, reality began to sink in
and Angus had an ironic thought; 'George, to this day had still
not killed a dragon'. Pyrra returned with Godroi limping badly,
but surprisingly able enough to fly. With Godroi's help, Angus
somehow managed to lay the broken knight across Pyrra's
back and they made their way slowly back to her lair once more
to recuperate.

It was not long after they reached her cave that the knight
returned to consciousness and groggily looked about the place.
He sat upright and began to converse with Godroi about the
battle and what had happened to the foe after he was knocked
out. Pyrra joined the conversation as she filled in the blanks
from what she had witnessed and what Angus had told her.
Apart from the burn and a massive bruise to his head, George
appeared to be in fine health and Angus was glad to see him
up and walking about. As Angus searched his own
recollections and thoughts of the events that had just occurred,

the realisation of what he had done hit him like a slap. The lad became quite troubled as it sank in; he had been the one to deal the death blow to the black dragon!

"You look upset Angus, are you okay?" asked Pyrra anxiously.

"Can we be sure that Felspar is actually dead?" asked Angus in reply. "Maybe he's just wounded somewhere and will come back for revenge!"

"Angus, there is no way he could have survived that wound" Pyrra soothed. "You split his heart stone in half and pierced his chest…. he could not still be alive!" she answered carefully.

Angus smiled wanly at her and nodded his agreement but was still unconvinced.

"Look, you did what had to be done! You saved the life of the Ward of the future and also that of George, the first dragon protector" she continued. "When it came down to it, only you were in a position to do that. By your actions you've secured the future of all dragons!"

Pyrra with her invisibility powers fully restored, thanks to her secret stash of Dragonore, flew back over the scene of the battle with Angus. She was anxious to put the lad's mind at rest and they searched the area finding the blood trail from

Felspar's wound. They followed a trickle of blood for about a mile until they met a stream in a small valley. The blood disappeared at the stream and after a quick search of the ground Angus spied some gems resting on the bottom of the sandy stream. This was proof enough that Felspar had died and self combusted just as Angus had witnessed in previous dragon deaths.

"His ashes have been washed away in the stream" said Pyrra.

"It's just some gemstones left… look there's his broken Dragonore!" added Angus pointing into the water.

Reassured that Felspar was truly dead, Angus still anguished over the fact that he had dealt the deathblow to the malicious dragon.

They returned to the cave to find that George was up and about and had made some sort of paste from plants he had found in the valley outside. The paste had been applied to Godroi's wounds and the golden dragon seemed all the better for it. Pyrra and Angus had stopped off at the rocky valley before the portal and dug up the Dragonore they had buried there. It was an idea Angus had, and would save them another trip to Krubera. The young protector had figured that they needed more Dragonore every time they passed through the portal. Three more trips to be exact, and on the earliest occasion when they went to awaken Barfoot, they took extra and buried it near the portal. Angus figured since they were as far back in time as they needed to go, it should still be there in the future.

"Halettan Pyrra... Halettan min beadurinc geong!" said George as they entered.

Angus recognised the term used by the knight and the man stood before him smiling broadly. Pyrra explained to Godroi and George what they had found during their search. He spoke to Pyrra and she told Angus that the knight wished to tell him something that she would translate.

"Angus, you have not only saved Godroi's life... and mine too for that matter..." she related as the knight's strong and deep voice spoke in Old English, "but undoubtedly your brave and selfless actions have saved the hierarchy of all dragons... You truly are a hero and deserve a reward and memento of this great occasion!"

The knight stooped and lifted his broken sword from the floor of the cave. He held it out and spoke again for Pyrra to repeat in modern English.

"I pledge that this sword will be re-forged and I will bury it between the pillars of Stanbury... One day in the future you

may need it and your sword will be there waiting for you!"
That said, the great Knight George knelt on one knee before
Angus and held the hilt of the sword for him to formally accept.
Pyrra for once was speechless and could only nod wordlessly
as her eyes glinted with tears. Angus took the proffered hilt,
deeply moved but at the same time awkwardly embarrassed by
the gesture.

Chapter 25

'Going Home'

After Godroi had sufficiently recovered enough to escort his old friend George to the gateway, the intrepid quartet flew to Marnham Church where the golden dragon chatted amiably on the grass in the churchyard. He added his grateful thanks to the others as he fully understood exactly what he could have lost.

Pyrra and Angus had still not revealed to him why he was so important and during their adventure Godroi had become very fond of Pyrra. The Knight George was highly amused by the picture in the stained glass window showing him as a dragon slayer, and Angus smiled as he recalled his thought from yesterday, but kept it to himself. However George proclaimed something lengthy in Old English.

"He said how funny it was to see his image depicted in such a victorious fashion when in fact it should be your features in the window, not his!" translated Pyrra for Angus.

Angus reddened in his embarrassment as he knew that through the course of time, the myth surrounding George and the dragon would become a total fabrication shaped by folklore and fairy tale. At that moment only four knew the truth of the matter and all took an oath of secrecy, solemnly swearing that the events of the day would be kept to themselves.

Before they could leave for home and their own century, Pyrra and Angus needed to escort George back to his time. With no villagers in sight they bade goodbye to Godroi and while the others spoke in Old English, Angus went to dig up the Dragonore from its hiding place. As he dug, he struggled with the idea that although he had just buried the stones the day before, they had been in the ground for over four hundred years! When he came back the knight held up his broken sword and reminded everyone present of his vow. After a brief translation from Pyrra, Angus wondered if he would ever receive the wonderful gift that would be left by the knight. Surely someone would find the treasure in the years that had to pass before Angus could get to it.

"Thank you" he replied bowing his head in respect to the armoured man before him.

Angus jumped onto Pyrra's back, as did George and after she picked up the extra Dragonore from the ground, she was off; her concentration aiming for later in the day they left with George in the year 798. Both riders waved to Godroi as he flew ahead of Pyrra, all were safe in the knowledge that he would remain in her lair until he was fully healed; the golden dragon falling slightly behind her as she accelerated towards the gateway. Angus once again marvelled at the experience of passing through the pillars, into the purple light, to be enveloped in time itself!

Chapter 26

'Precious Gift'

Early on a Saturday morning in mid October, two weeks after their return, Angus and Pyrra took off from Piggleston. Fully recovered from their time travelling adventures, the pair decided to go to the pillars once more and using the excuse of checking on the two dragons left on guard, they approached the portal at a steady pace.

"Caedmon... Argent... how are you doing... any sign of trouble?" asked Angus after dismounting from Pyrra's back. The guards had been placed at the portal just as a precaution and it seemed to be unwarranted as there had been no sign of Felspar.

"It seems he really is gone for good" concluded Pyrra. "Rathlin said you two can leave now... no use guarding this place forever... he's dead and that's the end of it. We'll catch up with you at Calmor"
The grey and silver dragons left for the impromptu celebration that everyone had been called to, on the island. No real reason was given for the meeting, but it was made absolutely clear that every dragon and protector should attend.

Angus cast his mind back to his adventure with Pyrra and

their subsequent finding of the Knight George as well as the battles with Felspar. Since then, they had been back to Krubera to check on Godroi and his recollection of the events and Angus remembered his secretive smile when he told them he always knew who Angus was, but how could he ever explain such a thing. Barfoot had been the same as even he had met both of them on two separate occasions many hundreds of years before. All Godroi knew was that only Pyrra could go back in time to save him and Angus had to go with her. Even Caedmon, the good one, remembered them and his reason for not saying anything was almost laughable. Angus could hear him saying 'but naturally I assumed you would remember me', which was all very well, except they had not met him in the same order of time he had met them. The young protector smiled as he recalled the confused look on the grey dragon's face when they tried to explain it to him and in the end they gave up. Despite the fact they had been victorious in their battle with Felspar and had managed to save the present, Angus felt a bit flat. Even the thought of his impending birthday was not enough to raise his spirits.

"Are you thinking about the sword?" asked Pyrra breaking into his reverie.

"Not really... just all the stuff that's happened, everything really…" replied Angus, sad that the adventure was over although extremely pleased by the outcome. "Do you think he left it?" he asked Pyrra.

"Perhaps he did… why don't you have a look around, after all it's your birthday next week and what better present could you ask for?" she smiled.

Angus stood for a few seconds, torn between the hope of finding his gift and fear of not; he stepped towards the tall stones.

The long grass and thistles between the pillars looked as if they had not been disturbed since the pillars were erected some five thousand or so years ago and Angus could not even contemplate the thought that anything would be there. He looked up at Pyrra and sensing his thoughts she used her left claw to scrape the area clear of the weeds. Angus produced a small garden trowel he had brought just in case and getting down on his knees, began to carefully scrape the earth away from the central area between the pillars. He dug down for several minutes and had found nothing but stones and dirt. Pyrra shuffled behind him as she felt the lad's disappointment grow with every scoop of earth. She recalled the moment they arrived back in George's time, and as Angus ran to get the spare Dragonore, the knight had once again reiterated his vow.

They had replaced his Dragonore that had been lost through time travel, but perhaps he in turn had not managed to replace the weapon or had died before he could fulfil his oath.

"Pyrra, I've hit something!" called Angus.

"What is it?" she asked hopefully.

Angus scrabbled with both hands at the dirt, not caring about the mess he was getting into with the damp soil. Suddenly he stopped and Pyrra thought he had been mistaken and found nothing more than a large rock. The young protector spun around and up at the same time, surprising her so much she stepped back to avoid him hitting her nose.

Angus held a long flat object covered in oily cloth, across the front of his body and Pyrra judged by his stance that it was heavy.

"Put it down and open it then!" she said excitedly.

Angus dropped to his knees and un-wrapped the object carefully as if it was made of glass or as fragile as an egg. The sunshine broke through the clouds just as the last piece of oilcloth was removed and the light glinted magically off the same sword that had destroyed Felspar. The great Knight George's weapon, wielded by the young protector Angus Munro! The sword had indeed been re-forged and Angus marvelled at the workmanship of the truly magnificent blade. The hilt was exactly as he remembered except for two minute details; an inscription and a jewel. The inscription was from George and was the same phrase he had used in honour of Angus; the jewel was one of the rarest and most precious stones on earth, Dragonore!

Chapter 27

'Celebration'

Just under two hours later, the duo reached Calmor, the last of the guests to arrive at the surprise gathering Rathlin had called. The head of the SSDP was keen to share some urgent and exciting Society news with protectors and dragons and had summoned them all to Calmor. They landed on the grass near the castle and approached the front entrance on foot as they had seen the underground cave entrance by the jetty was already congested with arriving dragons. As Angus watched the dragon-littered sky, he felt a familiar tingling sensation at the back of his neck and turned to see Georgina smiling up at him from a lower step.

"Hey Angus, what's the buzz? Any idea why we have all been summoned?" shouted Liam from behind her.

Angus had no idea and he knew it could not involve his recent adventure as that private celebration had already taken place on the Sunday night they arrived back. He recalled the way Georgina had run to him with the others. Unselfconsciously, she hugged and kissed him before he knew what had hit him. They had all listened intently around the campfire as Angus and Pyrra recollected the adventure, piece by exciting piece, leaving no detail untold.

"Sorry I'm as much in the dark as the rest of you!" he replied eventually.

"Did Argent bring you and your father?" Angus asked Georgina.

"No, I have a new dragon to protect now and he's moved into the stained glass window" she replied and pointed to a splendid looking male dragon. "His name is Wymarc!" Angus could see that Pyrra had already met the dark blue dragon at her favourite spot of Blue Dragon Fire. He could tell that she was getting on very well with the new dragon as they chatted amiably with Cyru and Cairistiona.

Whilst Angus and his friends stood with their back to the castle, Liam spotted the unusual package that the lad carried on his back.

"What's that then Angus?" asked the Irish lad.

"Oh… it's a sword!" he replied casually.

"COOL!" he shouted drawing the attention of too many other protectors. "Let's see it then!" Angus went bright red as he reluctantly un-strapped the heavy sword and placed it on one of the steps.

"Is that the one George promised you?" asked Georgina. Angus and Pyrra had kept their promise of silence about who had killed Felspar. The only others who knew the truth were Rathlin and Mrs T, but he guessed that Finian probably knew as well, and of course Godroi. Rathlin had thought it best if people believed that the knight had done the deed, and not Angus.

"Yes it is" he replied as the wrapping came free to reveal the shining blade in all it's glory!

"AWESOME!" the cry went up around him.

Rathlin, drawn to the noise being made by the younger members of the SSDP, walked over to see what all the fuss was about.

Rathlin looked over Georgina's shoulder and his mouth gaped at the beautiful weapon that lay on the steps of his castle.

"Well I'll be!" he exclaimed.

Angus feared that the white haired man would react badly to the sight of such a weapon at Calmor but instead heard;

"That's a fine sword you have there Angus and it's inscribed… 'Min beadurinc geong', what does it mean?"

"My young warrior" whispered Angus.

"Very apt… We shall have to find a safe place for you to keep it… can you take it home?"

"I guess not but I was hoping I could keep it here…" replied

Angus, "would that be okay?"

"I would be honoured to keep your sword safe at Calmor, and you're welcome to see it anytime you need to!" replied Rathlin smiling.

"That is so cool… you're so lucky Angus… I wish I had a sword like that… Can I hold it?" said Liam almost bouncing up and down on the spot.

The rest of the group laughed and once the overenthusiastic protector had held the historic weapon, Rathlin ushered them all into the Great Hall and down into the large cavern below.

Rathlin stood in the middle of the cave and with every dragon and protector present Angus was reminded of the Gathering for the choosing ceremony some months before. Rhys walked over beside the SSDP head and stood beside him positively glowing with pride. Rathlin did not keep them in suspense for long.

"My friends, I know you are wondering why I have brought you here…" as usual he scanned his audience, gleaning up the attentiveness from every face. "Some months ago Godroi, our revered Ward and keeper of the Cor Stan decreed that the time had come for all dragons to awaken. The time of hibernation needed to come to an end or dragon-kind would face extinction!" this statement caused a murmur from the dragons.

"He declared that your numbers must increase to prepare for the time that you may walk the earth free from attack and misunderstanding once again!" a cheer went up around the cavern, or as Angus perceived, a roar. "It is on that note and with great personal pleasure that I hand you over to the real star of this gathering, Rhys and her new additions to our ever growing family!"

Rathlin stepped back leaving Rhys in the limelight. Nobody had really paid her much attention up to that point and it was then that Angus noticed she carried two rugby ball sized ovals.

The silence that followed was strange as Rhys beamed at everyone gazing proudly at the two objects in her claws. She placed them very carefully on the ground in front of her and as Angus studied them he could hear some of the dragons begin to roar in approval. Angus looked to Pyrra for a clue.

"They're eggs Angus... dragon eggs!" she said, tears in her eyes. "The first dragon eggs to be laid since the end of the Great Hibernation and more importantly, the first clutch for over a thousand years!"

Everyone broke into spontaneous applause and Rhys the red dragon had a ruddier complexion than usual as she beamed at her audience and accepted their hearty congratulations.

Rathlin made a great speech befitting the momentous

occasion and bestowed upon her the name of 'Mæst Modor', meaning great mother. Angus managed to get a closer look when he finally got to meet Rhys.

"Can I touch one Rhys?" he asked politely.

"Of course you can Angus but please be careful" she replied smiling.

"Thanks" he replied.

"No, thank *you* Angus… without you, we would be lost in time and history!" she replied making him blush, especially when he realised Georgina stood next to him grinning. He bent to inspect the eggs, glad to avoid any further discomfiture, and noticed that they were almost flat at the base.

They were roughly oval-shaped with a thick veined pattern around them and they tapered to a blunt, rounded point at the top. They were pearlescent in colour, like the inside of a seashell and changed

colours when you moved your head from side to side.

"How long before they hatch?" he asked from his crouched position.

"Roughly twelve weeks" replied Rhys.

Angus decided he would have to sketch them later on. When he thought about all that had happened that day he decided that his impending thirteenth birthday would probably be the best yet.

During the celebrations, nobody noticed that one of the protectors had slipped out of the cavern. Silently and stealthily, the person sneaked their way up the dragon portrait-filled stairs and along the hallway to the Turret Room. This was the room that held all the important and confidential information on protectors and dragons alike, and was the inner sanctum of the SSDP. The infiltrator ran a long black gloved finger along the shelf they wanted and seemed to know exactly what they were looking for. The spy selected a file, pulling out a folder within it and spread the documents on the desk. Using a mobile phone, the mole started systematically taking pictures of the documents and after copying all the information in that particular file, they carefully replaced it. The intruder then went to the world map with its brightly coloured pins showing the locations of the awakened dragons, and after they removed the black gloves, began to photograph again, stopping only in alarm when the door clicked open quietly.

Meredith's immaculately manicured fingernails placed the phone in her handbag before she turned to greet the person who had just entered the room. She turned to see Aurora Tek, hands on hips, and extremely angry.

"What on earth are you doing?" asked Mrs T.
For a split second Meredith looked shocked but regained her composure so quickly Mrs T almost fell for it.

"Oh hello Aurora… I remembered something vital in a file and I just wanted to check…" replied Meredith brightly.
The dark haired protector tried to place her handbag on the table but nervously fumbled the bag over the edge and dropped it on the floor. The contents of the bag were revealed as they spilled over the wooden floor at Mrs T's feet. Aurora stooped to pick up the paraphernalia and noticed something odd. The hastily hidden mobile phone still had the last image Meredith had taken of the pin board and a notebook had fallen open with the inside exposed. Mrs T picked both of them up and began to read the pages accidentally revealed.

"Excuse me! That is private!" said Meredith frostily as she tried to take the items from Mrs T.
The wife of the SSDP head pulled the notebook away.

"I think I will be the judge of that dear!" she replied tersely.

Mrs T began to read the notes on the page she had found opened and it seemed to be the last entry in the book. As she quickly scanned the page filled with precise notes about Rhys' condition, she could see Meredith fidget nervously and then tap the top of her table with her fingernails. Mrs T read back a few pages and found notes on Angus, Pyrra and many others including a derogatory comment about Rathlin. She'd had enough of this woman and her fingernail tapping.

"Would you stop that infernal tapping!" she said loudly and firmly.

Meredith stopped and looked at her fingers on the table as if she had just seen them for the first time. Just then Rathlin walked in.

"Aurora my love are you in here?" he called.

When he saw the two women standing by the table eyeing each other unkindly he stopped dead in his tracks.

"What's going on?" he asked directing the question to his wife.

"I think Aurora has got the wrong idea about the contents of my harmless little notebook!" said Meredith cutting off Mrs T before she could answer her husband.

Aurora Tek looked furiously at the insolent woman before her and without a word she opened the notebook and handed it to

Rathlin. He began to read the entries and his expression changed from confusion to indignant hurt.

"But why would you… I don't understand!" he babbled.

"Read some more…" urged Mrs T, "It's all there… Angus, Pyrra… She's been making notes on everything and everyone!"

"Rathlin I can explain… Please, it's not what you think!" pleaded Meredith.

Rathlin ignored her and read, getting angrier as he flicked through the pages. Mrs T placed the final nail in the coffin for Rathlin to hammer home, by giving him the phone with the photo on it. He scrolled through the other pictures of the files and could see that Aurora had been right about the woman all along. Angus arrived just as Rathlin brusquely invited Meredith to sit at the table and explain her actions.

After several minutes shamelessly eavesdropping by the door, it was clear to the young dragon protector that even Meredith Quinton-Jones, a high powered oil and gas businesswoman who had been caught red handed, could not talk her way out of this one. They all knew what was to follow and sure enough Mrs T called for Rathlin, the head of the SSDP, who had always been supportive towards the strikingly handsome benefactress, to banish her from the Society. He was, by now, incandescent with rage having listened to her lies at the table and now realised he had been made to look like an idiot. He unceremoniously banished her from the SSDP and raged at her all the way down the stone stairs.

Meredith declined to speak, her face resolute, as she was escorted from the castle, the pictures from her camera phone having first been deleted and the notebook confiscated. Caedmon was summoned to fly her home and he was told that he would have to find a new home as he could no longer have anything to do with her.

"I will move back to Paris" he said unconcerned about the fuss.

"Tell your twin he will have to move also!" ordered Rathlin, after Angus whispered a reminder in his ear.

"Oh he has already gone to somewhere in Wales… never did tell me where, but he did say something about being disturbed all the time and not being able to sleep. He always was a little strange though!" replied the grey dragon before he took off with a stern-looking Meredith sitting on his back.

Rathlin shut the oak door firmly and bolted it for good measure in more of a symbolic gesture than to keep the woman from getting back in. He leant back against it, took his handkerchief from his breast pocket and wiped the sweat from his forehead. Angus had watched the scene in disbelief and a handful of other protectors had tagged along to witness the spectacle. He was shocked to realise that Meredith was the one who had passed on the information to Felspar. Why she had done it he had no idea; she had known one of the prime rules of the Society was preserving secrecy and what good would the files be to her anyway? Rathlin's puce face toned down to its more usual rugged complexion as he ushered Angus and his wife downstairs, brushing aside their anxieties and questions. He did not like being played for a fool.

"Come on, this is Rhys' day... lets not spoil it for her!"

Chapter 28

'Winter Chill'

Angus awoke in his bed at home in Kynton. He had not dreamt about dragons for ages, but had just been visited by the blue dragon in his sleep. He could not make out what the dream dragon had said and the whole thing puzzled him, leaving him with a familiar feeling of uneasiness. The usual sounds from outside seemed slightly muffled today; the cars sounded strangely subdued on the road and the postman's footsteps sounded like he had slippers on. Angus pulled the duvet down so his face was exposed and the air in his bedroom was distinctly chilly. Suddenly it dawned on him, and he leapt out of bed and peered out through the curtains. It was snowing! School was over for the holidays and soon it would be Christmas. With greater enthusiasm than usual, Angus dressed faster than he did when putting on his school uniform. He hurtled outside and although the flakes were beginning to settle he thought there probably was not enough to prevent him from cycling to Piggleston and back. He pedalled for a short distance, gingerly applied the brakes and skidded satisfyingly on the icy road.

He found Pyrra shivering in the high street and a bit

downcast as she had not seen any children for days. It was much too cold to be having rides in the winter or giving them for that matter. She had been thinking about flying off to her lair for some shelter, but brightened when she saw Angus come out of the sweet shop with the familiar paper bag.

"Good to see you Angus… this cold weather is awful and I think the snow is keeping the children away" she moaned with a mouthful of sweet.

"I wonder how Rhys is doing… we should go and visit her and perhaps we might take her some of those" she motioned to the cough candy sweets he was holding.

Suddenly Angus had a moment of clarity, like a mist clearing in his mind, in his dream he had seen Rhys' eggs and the blue dragon silently mouthing something to him, but nothing more. He explained his bewilderment to Pyrra and she reminded him that the eggs were due to hatch in January, only one month away and not long now to wait.

"That must be what it's about" said Angus thoughtfully, "Nothing more than a reminder that Rhys' twins were due very soon."

He could hardly wait to see the newborn dragons and wondered what colour they would be. He stood on the pavement and chatted to Pyrra for a while longer before he watched her morph out of the children's ride and rise up through the snowflakes. She flew over the rooftops of Piggleston, heading off for the warmth of her cave for a couple of weeks, leaving her alter shell and the diminutive figure of Angus behind. There was no way he would be going with her, as he certainly did not want to skip Christmas. Georgina was coming to visit him and anyway he did not think for one minute that the dragon would be alone in her lair.

On the other side of the country, dressed entirely in black, a woman was talking animatedly into the phone whilst drumming her fingernails on the desk with her free hand. Eventually she hung up and walked around a large glass cased model of an oil rig with three latticework legs and a variety of structures protruding from it at various angles. She looked out from the old fashioned sash window that reflected the age of the Victorian building in which she stood. The window was one of three but the blinds were closed on the other two. The dark haired woman gazed unseeing across the view of the Thames with the London Eye, Canary Wharf and beyond to Big Ben with the Houses of Parliament below. As she continued her tapping on the glass case she glared at her fingers and then she spoke in a very low, icily cold voice,

"How dare they kick me out of their silly little society!" she scowled.

All this took place in the plush offices of QJ Drilling Limited and Meredith was still not happy about her dismissal some months previously. Until now, she had been able to avoid the subject; but her visitor had reminded her of the most embarrassing and painful humiliation of her cosseted life.

She paced the room and continued to berate the SSDP and also herself, for being so careless. Her voice rose in intensity but not in volume, which made it all the more scary as she vowed revenge on the Tek family and the whole Society of Dragon Protectors, secret or not. Then she smiled;

"Of course they think they stopped me by taking away my notebook... But I can remember all too well what was written and coupled with the files removed from Rathlin's desk before that, I have more than enough to move forward with our plans" she said.

Meredith turned and addressed a dark and shadowy corner of the room.

"So, how did you manage to get back?" she asked.

"Ha! That was easy... I scraped a few jewels off my chest and dropped them in the stream, leaving the water to do the rest. The blood was genuine but I was not defeated and I will not die at their hands" growled the voice. "I fooled them all and that lazy green female dragon didn't even bother to search properly. She and the meddlesome boy believed I was slain... I picked up the broken Dragonore later and found it still had its special powers and that allowed me to hide from danger, inserting it back into my wounded chest... It was some time before I was fit enough to fly but believe me, someone will pay for the pain I endured that day, and for the days since!" the voice spat, full of venomous hatred and loathing.

Meredith screwed her face up and leaned forward as she jabbed her finger in the direction of the voice, the room arced and sparked with ill feelings of malevolence and revenge. She spoke with an icy chill in her voice and there was no mistaking her meaning.

"I don't care how you do it... just get the two of them!"

Nothing was visible in the dark corner of the room, until out from the shadow a light appeared. It was the menacing glint of a glowing red eye.

List of dragons found so far

Pyrra	Oswin
Godroi	Leofric
Argent	Nehebkau
Rhys	Macklin
Nathair	Felspar
Cyru	Piran
Grimbald	Wyma
Kendrick	Alwin
Hildred	Caedmon
Galfridus	Radulf
Swithin	Eoghan
Sperling	Hereward
Beorn	Barfoot
Caedmon	Tejas
Walkelin	Wymarc
Uchtred	Cairistiona
Gilmor	Erantha
Farrell	Devansh
Wolfstanus	Slivier
Angharad	

Lexicon of Old English

Ac - And	Freonds - Friends
Arweorðe - Honourable	Geong - Young
Beadurinc - Warrior	Halettan - Hello
Becuman - Come	Ic - I
Byrigan - Taste	Iren - Steel
Cunnan - Know	Mæst Modor - Great Mother
Don - Do	Min - My
Duguð - Warband	Noht - Not
Eow - You	Ond - And
Forstandan - Understand	Thegn - Knight

Glossary

Cairn – Heap of stones set up as a landmark

Dragonore or Heart Stone – The precious stone that enables dragons, and their protectors, to recognise each other.

Dragon time – A power used by a dragon to speed up or slow time.

Dolmen – A stone structure, usually a tomb with two standing stones and one across the top.

Henge – An ancient monument of the British Isles; usually a circle enclosed by bank and ditch, with upright stones or pillars.

Great Hibernation – The name used by dragons to describe their enforced hiding until such a time they deem the earth a safe place to once again inhabit.

Megalith – A stone of massive size used in ancient construction work.

Monolith – A single massive stone.

Morphing or to morph – A verb used by dragons to describe their transformation into an inanimate object.

Portal – Doorway or gateway.

Fitbaw – Scottish slang for football.

Hame – Scots word for home.

Pehs – Dundee colloquialism for pies.

Twa – The number two.

Since he started writing with Debi, John has discovered a lot about his own abilities, and by self publishing the books, he has pushed his skills to new heights. His vivid imagination has helped to create the world of the SSDP and with the ability to produce the same depth of perception in his illustrations he has brought life to the characters' and locations described within. Since many other story ideas are brimming in his subconscious, John is looking forward to continuing his journey with Angus and Pyrra as they travel on many future adventures.

Debi, always a firm believer, has gone dragon mad and is seeing potential hiding places everywhere, since embarking upon this writing adventure. Researching this book gave her an excuse to hug stones, another secret passion. Debi enjoys going into schools to introduce children to the SSDP and makes no secret of the fact that she loves being recognised in supermarkets! She would love to see one of her own drawings in the book but alas, she can only draw stick men with turned up toes and sheep. Debi has an obsession with semi colons and exclamation marks and still has a problem ending a sentence. Perhaps this will improve by the end of the series!

Look out for book six in the series.

THE SECRET SOCIETY
OF
DRAGON PROTECTORS

Coming Soon!

For further details visit the official SSDP website at

www.thesecretsocietyofdragonprotectors.com